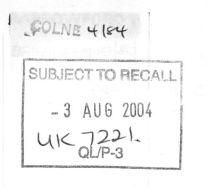
AUTHOR	CLASS No.
BENTINE, M	F
MADAME'S GIRLS, AND OTHER STORIES	
	98011792

D0783553

X

G

Madame's Girls

and other Stories

Madame's Girls

and other Stories

MICHAEL BENTINE

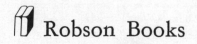

Robson Books

FIRST PUBLISHED IN GREAT BRITAIN IN 1980 BY
ROBSON BOOKS LTD., 28 POLAND STREET,
LONDON W1V 3DB. COPYRIGHT © 1980 MICHAEL
BENTINE.

British Library Cataloguing in Publication Data

Bentine, Michael
   Madame's girls, and other stories
   I. Title
   823.'9'1FS   PR6052.E54/

   ISBN 0-86051-122-7

01861067

Reproduced from copy supplied
printed and bound in Great Britain
by Billing & Sons Limited
Guildford, London, Oxford, Worcester

Contents

All these stories have a basis in my own experience. They wrote themselves in one intense session of three months but I suppose I have been writing them in my head for the last thirty years. There is a border line in the memory where it is very difficult to sift fact from fiction, and these stories inhabit that area. However, any resemblance to actual persons, living or dead, is purely coincidental, and all names are fictitious.

M.B.

Who Can You Tell?

FIRST OF ALL, let me say that I'm very glad you came to me, because I do feel that I am your closest friend – and, after all, what is a close friend for?

Secondly, I'm glad that you haven't told anyone else about your experience! I am the first person that you've told – right?

Good! Not that I'm saying that another person wouldn't believe you, but let's face it, you've got to be very much on the same wave-length to accept the story you've just told me without questioning the state of mind you were in when you came here.

Of course, because of our long friendship – let's see now, it's almost twenty years – Yes! Twenty years of *close* friendship, not only in business but also on a personal level – I believe you! Why? As I say, because of real friendship! Based on mutual trust and respect.

Naturally you came to me, out of your many friends, and I do feel very flattered that you have put me in such a unique position of trust and confidence. However – and please

don't take this in the wrong way – I do feel that I would be
failing in my duty as a close friend and business associate if
I didn't sound a warning note.

This whole experience of yours, although it is strange
- in fact weird! – is still not altogether without precedent.
After all, people have been seeing lights in the sky and other
unidentified flying objects for years. Ever since the written
word became commonplace, Man has been seeing and even
hearing things probably just as mind-bending – oh sorry! I
didn't mean you to take me literally – just a figure of speech!
Well, I mean to say, you are the sanest person I know –
certainly not unbalanced in any way – so when I said 'mind-
bending' I just meant – for the *ordinary* man.

Now I've always considered you an *extra*ordinary man,
and when *you* say that you've seen and experienced something then I sit up and take notice – without question!

Still, you have been working very hard – as usual, I might
add – but especially during these last few weeks, very hard
indeed, and after all is said and done, you're – I mean, *we're*
– not as young as we were – right? Right!

So there is a possibility – and mind you, I'm only saying
a possibility, not a probability – that you might have mis-
taken some unusual natural phenomenon for what you felt
you saw and – correct me if I'm wrong – thought you heard.

Now, before you fly off the handle, hear me out! Don't
think for one moment that I'm doubting you. Your word is
your bond! I fully accept that. But there are one or two quite
rational explanations for what you took to be lights in the
sky. A morning star seen through moving clouds – or clouds
themselves – on a frosty morning can reflect lights from a
distant city or even sunlight shining on glass, a long way off.
Then there's mirages. Don't forget them! After all, we've
both seen them in the course of our much-travelled lives, eh?

What about shooting stars? Admittedly, not too common
in the daylight, but still a possibility.

Then there's the voice! Or what sounded to you like a

voice. You told me yourself that when you heard it you fell down – or rather that you fell down when you were blinded by the light – and *then* you heard it! Yes, I think those were your exact words.

Could it have been the sudden brightness of the sun coming from behind thick clouds, just after you came out of that shady tree-lined bit of the road where you say that it happened? Ah! Now there's a thought.

How's this for an idea? You saw the light – it blinded you! You lost your balance and fell! Hit your head on a rock! Remember, you had a nasty cut on your temple when you arrived on my doorstep, and you were dazed – decidedly groggy, I thought. In fact it took you quite a while to calm down. I distinctly remember I gave you a glass of wine because you looked so bad, and it did take a while before you were coherent enough to tell me what had happened.

I'm not saying that the whole thing happened in your imagination! *No!* I'm just saying that it *could* have done so, given some of the circumstances that I've just suggested.

Anyway, I wouldn't be a real friend if I didn't tell you, to the best of my ability, what I think is best for you in the circumstances.

Please don't get me wrong when I say: before you tell anyone else, go back home – never mind the urgent business appointment that you were on your way to keep, that can wait a day or two. But first, take my advice – sleep on it, in your own home – and when you wake up in the morning, I'm sure that you'll know what to do about it.

You're a very well-respected businessman and a much admired citizen, and people trust in you and your judgement and come from miles around to consult you and do business with you. Think of the effect it will have – your going around with a story like this. *Of course* I believe you, because I know you so well – but others may not be so ready to accept what you say. So please think very carefully before you breathe a word of this to anyone else!

After all, why should 'they', whoever 'they' are, choose to contact you – of all places – right slap-bang in the middle of the road to Damascus?

Go back home to Tarsus, Saul, and just ask yourself: *Who can you tell?*

Madame's Girls

'AND BOYS,' added the Senior Milkman, 'Madame has a number of boys at the school. It's co-educational – best ballet school in England, so they say!'

The supposedly silent electric milk van clattered and bounced its shuddering way over the rutted, ill-kept drive of the neglected estate that housed Madame Marashkova's school of Russian Ballet, Yoga and General Education. The Junior Milkman sat in awe beside the rotund, ruddy-faced, luxuriantly-moustached Mr Blossom, who was initiating him into the mysteries of a country milk delivery service.

'I always like to finish off my round with Madame,' Mr Blossom declared sagely. 'A very remarkable woman, and a very fine ballet teacher – so Deirdre says – and she's very happy there!'

'How long has your daughter been at the school?' enquired the lean, sallow-faced, young milkman, clinging grimly to the rattling milk van as it bounced from pot-hole to pot-hole.

'About two years now. Done her a power of good –

slimmed her down no end – and put paid to her acne!
Marvellous thing, ballet!'

'Must cost you a packet?'

'Well, Madame and I have an arrangement. She gives my
Deirdre ballet lessons at a reduced rate – thinks the world of
her, does Madame. Called her a "cheerful, willing pupil" in
her last report. 'Course, she's a bright girl, my Deirdre –'

At that moment a wild whoop sounded on the crisp
morning air, and the Junior Milkman's amazed eyes were
treated to the spectacle of an apparently riderless horse
thundering across the field towards them. Before he could
frame an astonished question, Mr Blossom explained:
'Cossacks, Alfred, Cossacks.'

Just as it seemed that the black fury of the racing horse
was about to jump the broken fence which bordered the
gravel drive and land on top of the milk van in a crash of
broken bottles, a head appeared over its neck, followed by a
pair of long Russian-booted legs, which swung the now-
visible rider over the horse's back and firmly seated him in
the saddle. As he regained his balance, he swerved his
speeding mount aside and, with a display of consummate
horsemanship, pulled the large black horse up into a rearing
halt. Alfred gaped up at the rider, a grey-haired man with a
grizzled Van Dyke beard.

'Morning, Colonel Poliakoff!' shouted Mr Blossom
cheerily, as the elderly rider trotted his sweating steed beside
the milk van.

'Good morning, Blossom,' the Cossack Colonel replied in
a parade ground voice, now slightly shrill with age. 'Cream
and yoghurt for me, please!'

As the milkman nodded, the Cossack expertly swung his
black charger round to face the opposite side of the field and,
crouched low over the horse's neck, galloped off across the
grass, unsheathing a long sword from its saddle-mounted
scabbard. The astonished Alfred's gaze followed the dashing
one-man charge as, speeding through a small clump of

saplings set in the middle of the field, Colonel Poliakoff neatly sliced off two branches on either side of him.

'The Colonel's a bloody marvel at that trick riding lark!' commented Mr Blossom admiringly. 'Nice to see him up and about again!'

'Hasn't he been well?' Alfred managed to ask, without taking his eyes from the disappearing horse and its rider.

'Well, he hasn't been *ill* exactly, but he fell a bit heavy during the display he and his mates gave at the school garden party. Tent pegging, he was – bloody incredible how them old Russian geezers do it! Taking tent pegs out of the ground with a long lance while galloping along flat out! The Colonel broke his leg. Happens all the time.'

'He must be bloody unlucky!'

'No, Alfred, I mean it happens all the time to the Cossacks at the school – not just the Colonel. They're always laid up with something bust! I tell you, Alfred, it's bleeding dangerous, that Cossack lark!'

'What *do* they do it for then?' queried the mystified Alfred. 'Don't they have no regular jobs? Sounds bloody silly to do it as a hobby.'

'Oh, they've all got regular work, mate. The Colonel does all the school painting and decorating – another of 'em's a bank clerk – another one's a boot repairer. They do all sorts of jobs.'

'How old is he – the Colonel?'

'About seventy-five, I should say. His mates range from about seventy-eight down to the youngest – and he can't be a day under sixty-seven. That's why they keep hurting themselves – too bloody old, all of 'em!'

'Then why do they carry on like that?' Alfred persisted.

'Because they're Russian Cossacks, mate – mad as bloody March hares.'

As Mr Blossom pronounced his judgment (which wasn't too far from the truth), the milk float crunched to a stop on the gravelled forecourt outside the entrance to the Marashkova School of Russian Ballet. Alfred's eyes took in the fine, eighteenth-century mansion, with its grey plaster-rendered frontage cracking for want of a general face-lift. He swung his thin legs down from the van, and proceeded to the rear of the vehicle.

'How many?'

'Sixty pints of pasteurized – two dozen gold top – ten cartons of cream – ten pounds of butter – and twelve dozen eggs.'

'Not forgetting yoghurt!' called a high, sing-song voice, apparently coming from the cloud-pocked sky above.

Alfred looked up at the windows, searching for the giver of the yoghurt order, but could see no one. Mr Blossom, however, knew where to look, and shouted back: 'We're out of fruit yoghurt, but I'll leave ten dozen plain and Mrs Fenning can mix 'em up with garden fruit! All right?'

'Have you honey, Mr Blossom?' continued the voice, which Alfred now traced as coming from the roof of the school, where a tall, wiry, almost totally naked Indian was poised precariously on the crumbling stone parapet, one arm clutching the swaying end of the school fire escape. Reassured about his honey supply, the emaciated Indian withdrew from sight, and a high-pitched, rhythmical chant piped up over the roof-top.

'Professor Karma,' explained Mr Blossom, 'doing his orisons – I think that's what Deirdre calls 'em – anyway, greeting the day with prayers! He's very good at it – Deirdre says he's cured her constipation! Bloody marvellous! A bleedin' wizard, 'e is!'

While Alfred wondered at these strange phenomena, Mr Blossom deftly piled the wire-caged milk bottles at the side of the front door, which, surprisingly for such an imposing building, was only graced by one long, worn, white stone step; then the milkman hauled hard down on an iron bell-pull.

Somewhere deep in the bowels of the great house a distant

bell sounded, and shortly afterwards a door slammed hollowly and the scuffling of fast-moving, soft-shoed feet could be heard approaching the front door. A noisy latch and a heavy, reluctant bolt later, the weathered walnut door creaked open and a delicately-featured ballet dancer in a faded practice leotard and tights leaned gracefully out. A languid hand waved a greeting, and the long eyelashes fluttered beneath lank brown hair encased in a nylon stocking. It was hard to tell the sex of the willowy student. Nor did the shrill soprano voice help to clarify the situation for Alfred, as its owner piped up: 'Och, it's the Milky! I'll help you in with the bottles.'

The supple, black-clad grace of the figure belied an astonishing strength as the student effortlessly lifted two wire containers, each loaded with twelve pints of milk, and whisked them up through the front door as if they weighed nothing.

The young dancer reached for the next load, but Mr Blossom coughed discreetly and said firmly: 'There's two weeks to pay, Dougal. Fifty-two quid.'

'Is there now? Well, I'll tell Mrs Fenning. Won't be a minute!' The boy's broad Glaswegian accent clashed totally with his almost feminine grace and apparent frailty. Alfred gawped.

'By the way, Dougal,' said Mr Blossom as the dancer made a movement to withdraw, 'this is Alfred, my assistant. He'll be delivering while I'm away on holiday. How's Deirdre?'

'She's fine! At class at the moment – I'll give her your love! Hello, Alfred. Och, you're a nice wee boy!'

Dougal batted his luscious eyelashes seductively at the embarrassed Alfred, whose tall, skinny frame and bespectacled face hardly fitted the Scots boy's description – then, with a beautifully executed grand jeté, he vanished through the open doorway in the full character of the Spectre of the Rose which he was currently rehearsing.

The older milkman grinned, 'You'll get used to it, mate.'
'He was a bloke! Blimey! I thought he was a bird at first.'
'Strong as a bleeding horse,' stated Mr Blossom suc-
cinctly. 'These kids are athletes, Alfred! Ballet dancing may
look all airy-fairy but it makes muscles – so Deirdre says!'

While the two milkmen were discussing the interesting
features of the Marashkova School of Russian Ballet, Dougal
had flitted lightly through the panelled entrance hall, turned
left at the end with a neat pirouette, and piquéd gracefully
down the long, stone-flagged corridor beyond, till he arrived, with a final double tour-en-l'air and a perfect plié, with
scarcely a sound, in front of a dark mahogany door at the
end. Extending a well-positioned hand in a graceful arc, he
lightly knocked on the top panel.

After a moment the door was opened by a small, plump,
prematurely grey-haired woman whose friendly face was
brightened by a pair of shrewd, amused eyes. She greeted
him with a smile. 'Dougal – what is it, dear? I'm a bit tied
up, so make it snappy!'

'The Milky's outside, Mrs Fenning, and he wants his
money just now. Och, and he's brought his young friend
with him. His name's Alfred and he'll be delivering milk
when Mr Blossom goes on holiday. Can I have it please –
fifty-two quid!'

'Tell Mr Blossom that I'll have the money for him in a
moment. I'm just going to get it from Madame. In the
meantime, ask him if he'd like to bring in his friend to
watch Deirdre in Class.'

Glasgow's answer to Nureyev, who had been standing
attentively in a perfect fifth position, plié-ed deeply and
performed a one-and-a-half tour-en-l'air to position himself
facing the other way down the corridor.

Then, in a series of highly elevated grand jetés, he sprang
athletically down the passage, performed another pirouette-
et-demie at the end, cartwheeled through the entrance hall,
straightened up, and back-flipped himself dramatically

through the front door, landing neatly and soundlessly on the worn front step to confront the duly impressed milk-men with their invitation to the ballet class.

While he led them in through the entrance hall, past the bronze statue of Anna Pavlova in her famous role as the Dying Swan, Madame's daughter Anna – now Mrs Nat Fenning – hurried upstairs to tap gently on the door of Madame's bedroom-study.

'Mother, can I see you for a moment?' Anna spoke in a clear, soft voice, deliberately muted even though it was projected sufficiently loudly to penetrate the thick wood of the door. A commanding voice answered her, and Anna quietly opened the door and stepped inside the high-ceilinged room.

'Annushka! You disturb me, darling! What is it you want?'

Although Madame and her daughter spoke Russian, during term-time they used only English or French. Madame spoke the latter both volubly and perfectly, the former rather quaintly, while Anna spoke both languages with equal fluency and with excellent grammar, and her extensive vocabulary encompassed a rich variety of swear words which she was careful never to use in her mother's presence. Madame never swore in public, except piously to invoke the deity in one of the many forms that she wor-shipped, and she never tolerated swearing in her hearing.

'It's the milkman, Mother. He wants to be paid.'

'Is imperative?' queried Madame Marashkova, who was standing comfortably on her head with her legs neatly locked together above her.

'I'm afraid so, Mother. Mr Blossom is terribly good, and if he says he must be paid, well, he must!'

'Pity Deirdre is not better dancer,' said the inverted Madame. 'But Mistair Blossom is natural gentleman – he must be paid! Minute, darling.'

With a grace and agility born of long practice, the great
Russian ballet teacher adroitly reversed her position and,
limping slightly with the painful arthritis which she never
allowed to interfere with her profession made her way to a
large chest of drawers. She selected a key from a chain
round her neck and opened the top one. From it she took
out a handbag of truly heroic proportions, once chic but
now somewhat battered, and extracted from it a wallet-
purse attached to a short chain.

'How much is?' Madame queried, rummaging about until
her hands were full of bank notes of various denominations
and a number of currencies.

'Fifty-two pounds, exactly!' said Anna firmly.

Madame's beady, bright eyes raised themselves dramatically to heaven. 'Dear God! Is robbery of children! My girls
and boys must have energy! Milk is energy! Milk tradesmen
charge blood money for milk. Is terrible price for something cow gives for nothing!'

Anna clucked sympathetically, but continued in her line
of argument. 'Mother, Mr Blossom is simply marvellous!
He charges us half what anyone else would and puts it
down to breakages. But he must have his money now, he's
stalled the Dairy long enough. We cannot expect him to
pay for it himself.'

'I know, Annushka darling! Dear God in Heaven – He
knows that I am patient – but Deirdre will never make good
dancer – she is heavy like cow! She has elevation of dancing
snake. But – milk is milk! And Blossom is good man. Pay
him, darling!' she finished dramatically, handing an assorted
bundle of crackling notes to her daughter. 'Fifty dollars
American – one hundred Deutsch marks – five hundred old
francs – ten pounds sterling – is all I have till I go to the
bank!'

Anna wished fervently that her mother were more conventional in her business dealings, but there was little that
she could do because those parents who did pay usually

handed over the fees in cash, and as they came from every
corner of the globe, the payments were in many different
currencies. Fortunately Mr Blossom understood the situation, and as his brother-in-law was a local bank clerk, he
managed to get the money changed at the current rate
without too many formalities. Furthermore the daughter of
the bank manager was Madame's head girl, so for the time
being this somewhat unusual arrangement worked perfectly
well.

As Anna left to conclude the international business deal
with the obliging milkman, Madame Natalia Marashkova
replaced her handbag in the chest of drawers, and turned to
a large bronze bust of a shaven-headed man with a strong,
sensitive face. The sculptor had caught the imperious artistic
arrogance in the half-turned, beautifully-proportioned head
that Madame gazed at attentively.

'Sergei,' she said matter-of-factly, as though she was
addressing the living subject of the sculptor's art, 'Sergei,
my darling! What is to be done?'

As was her habit when beset by anxiety, Madame shared
it with the bust of her late and much loved husband, Sergei
Ivanovitch Marashkov, of the Imperial Russian Ballet,
and soloist to the Czar Nicholas. She cradled the sun-
warmed head with its greeny-brown patina in her still-
lovely arms, and gently touched the shaven bronze scalp
with her lips.

'We are in some small financial difficulty, mon ange!'

Natalia Kulianov, whom Sergei had made Madame
Marashkova, on these occasions adopted the coquettishly
wheedling tone that she had so effectively employed when
her husband was alive, in order to win him over to her side
after committing some misdemeanour with the family house-
keeping, at which she was quite hopeless.

'Sergei, you must find us more money! Some parents of
the children live so far away and can only send money in
small amounts. Some parents don't pay till long time after

school reopens from holidays. We cannot turn away
talented boys and girls. Please, my darling, we need one
thousand pounds immediately – parce que nous sommes
dans la merde – jusqu'à là!'

Madame graphically illustrated, with her hand up to her
throat, just how far into the fertilizer the school had sunk.
Then, suddenly, she laughed the lovely thrilling laughter
of a young girl, her dark-brown eyes sparkling like onyx.

'Sergei! Do you remember when we had no money in
Paris? How you danced outside the Opéra, and we collected
twenty francs in your hat! Oh mon Dieu! What days they
were! You were gros gosse, mon ange!'

Madame broke off from her happy reminiscence and
threw herself down on her knees before a small shrine of
the Blessed Virgin which stood in the corner of her
bedroom-study. The beautiful old ikon was placed next to
a bronze buddha of inscrutable mien and ancient Chinese
craftsmanship. Beside this sat a statue of the Lord Shiva
and then, perched on various pieces of furniture or securely
fixed around the white walls of the sun-filled room, came a
succession of saints, idols, mandalas, tattvas, ikons, ser-
pents, dragons, Greek gods and Chaldean godesses, bronze
figures of Isis and Horus, and, finally, a large faïence
Ushabti next to a magnificent jade figure of Kwan-Yin. Had
Madame sold them at auction they would have realized ten
times the sum she was now earnestly praying for, but such a
solution would have been unthinkable: this diverse
collection of sacred archetypes was Natalia Marashkova's
guarantee of a quick passage to Heaven, in order that she
might be reunited with her adored Sergei.

A knock at her door interrupted Madame towards the end
of her prayers, and, crossing herself unhurriedly in the
manner of the Russian Orthodox Church, she rose from her
knees with an imperious: 'Who is?'

'Nat!' announced a strong, masculine voice from the
corridor. 'I must speak to you, Madame!'

'Come,' said Madame, and the door opened to admit the tall, slightly stooped, but broad-shouldered figure of her son-in-law, Nat Fenning.

The great ballet teacher smiled fondly at the humorous, worldly-wise face of her beloved Anna's husband, for she was genuinely happy at her only child's choice of a spouse. Nat, with his cheerful Cockney-Jewish temperament and down-to-earth commonsense, was extremely shrewd and well educated – largely by his own efforts – and, being a natural scholar, had taken to the intricacies of the ballet world like a rabbinical student to the Talmud. It was largely his quick thinking and resourcefulness that kept the school out of trouble.

This time Nat was the bearer of alarming news: the School Inspector was due to arrive at noon that very day. The significance of this piece of information was that the school had, as yet, despite its considerable length of operation, not been recognized by the education authorities. Such recognition would bring great financial relief to the beleaguered establishment, which only just stayed afloat through the constant inspired manoeuvering of Madame's oddly effective intuition, and Nat's shrewd business ability – and in spite of Madame's generosity in handing out scholarships to bright young dancers.

'Why is it not till now that you tell me this, Nat?' demanded his mother-in-law. She, above all, recognized the full import of the unexpected news.

'The letter was delayed by the postal strike, Madame,' replied Nat patiently, as always adopting the formal mode of address to the school's Director during school hours.

'Is disaster! This evening we have Ballet Concours at Hastings. The school bus must leave with the boys and girls at three o'clock promptly! Now Annushka and you, Nat, cannot go! You will have to stay and look after things for School Inspector.' A thought struck her. 'How is headmaster?'

'Not too well, Madame.'

'Where is he?'

'Sleeping it off, I'm afraid – he hit the bottle last night.'

'Nat, is last time! School Inspector will want to see headmaster – you must get him sober!'

'Very well, Madame, I'll do my best.'

The subject in question was a fully qualified and highly academic Scot, who had taken to drink after his wife had died. He also suffered from rheumatism, and this was another reason why he often sought solace in whisky.

'Head girl will have to take children to Hastings! Send Pamela to me immediately!'

'Right away, Madame. I'll get the other boys and girls organized. I'll put it to them straight: if they don't co-operate – that's the end of the school. Leave it to me, Madame. We'll pull it off somehow!'

If anyone could carry it off, Nat could! thought Madame as, once more alone, she turned back to the bust of her husband.

'You see, Sergei,' she said almost triumphantly, '*ils ne passeront pas!*'

Sergei gazed back with his unchanging expression of stern command, and his wife once again kissed the top of his smooth, dully shining head.

Downstairs, Nat had already gathered together the senior girls and boys and, before summoning the full quota of the formidable Marashkova family, was putting the position to the pupils simply and honestly.

There was a gasp from the polyglot assembly of bright young people, for there was as strong a bond of loyalty between Madame and her pupils, as between Madame and her family. Many of the seniors were there on sufferance because of Madame's love of talent, and all wanted to continue their almost fanatically concentrated ballet training in such wonderfully sympathetic surroundings. Their quickness of intellect and intensive physical training gave them an advantage over another, more conventional school faced with the same situation. Furthermore, they were aware of Madame's financial situation as this was reflected in many small economies in lighting and heating – though never in their food, which was always plentiful, well-cooked and imaginatively conceived. They were quite used to Dim Sims, paella, chicken Vindaloo and Nasi Goreng, pirochkis and borscht, such international dishes being served just as often as porridge and shepherd's pie.

The kitchen was presided over by Babushka, Madame's small and ancient mother, whose energy was still amazing at eighty, and whose English was non-existent. Her instructions, praises and curses were all delivered in a voluble mixture of Russian and French. With her scarf tied Slavic-style round her head, this formidable – sometimes ferocious – little woman somehow managed, with help from Anna and the girls, to produce a constant supply of tasty, energy-giving hot food for her ever hungry children – as she lovingly thought of them.

Pamela, the head girl and local bank manager's daughter, was a great favourite with Madame, not because of the obvious advantage of her well-placed father, but for the simple reason that she was a fine dancer.

'Pamela, darling, is important that you keep up girls' and boys' morale for Hastings Concours. Anna and Nat cannot go with, so you must be in charge.

'This year we will win all prizes. Usually we win gold medal – but I feel here in my heart that this time is gold, silver and bronze – we clear the bread board!

'Bus driver is Mistair Thompson – very careful old man – but you must see that he does not make you late! Good girl, Pamela! I place you in command – *in loco parentis* – yes?'

Madame had complete faith in Pamela but this was, after all, the first time that the head girl had undertaken a school outing, and such an important one at that, without parental or teacher supervision. Pamela Bushell – a lovely, faun-like seventeen-year-old, whose slender features gave an immediate impression of dependability, mixed with that elfin quality of indefinable charm which the French call 'gamine'.

'Don't worry, Madame. I'll look after everything,' she said, with all the conviction of her seventeen years, ten of which had been spent in dedicated study with her beloved teacher.

Madame kissed her on both cheeks, gently and with great affection.

'You are good girl, Pamela,' she said again. 'Now hurry, darling! Inspector is due to arrive midday. It is now – ' she consulted a small fob-watch which she wore on her dress, 'exactly ten o'clock. There is much to do – dormitories are big problem! We must move some beds in order not to seem so full!

'Tidy up everything, Pamela, and maybe – with God's help! – we will get good report from Inspector, and then school will get big fat grant! We need new studio and dormitories and classrooms and the good-God-knows-what!'

Pamela promised to do her best and rushed off to supervise the redistribution of the dormitory furniture. This problem of over-crowding was solely due to Madame's kindness of heart and the many scholarship pupils that the school carried. Accommodation was so limited that one pupil even lived in a cupboard .

The old studio floor badly needed re-laying and re-covering with new lino, and the classrooms were jam-packed and must soon be extended. All this would be immediately evident to the Inspector and might well fail them, when it came to the grant, but the biggest worry that the school had was the deficiencies in its academic programme.

Somehow the staff – consisting of Madame, Anna, Nat, Professor Karma, Colonel Poliakoff (when not decorating), and the headmaster (when sober) – managed to instil

enough knowledge of the basic subjects to get their pupils
through 'O' levels and even 'A' levels in languages and
other non-scientific subjects, but only because the pupils
realized that they must show reasonable academic progress
or the school would have to close, and that would be the end
of their ballet training.

While the school set about getting ready for the Inspector,
Madame descended the great staircase, the first landing of
which divided the boys' and girls' dormitories in either
wing of the house, with Madame's own bedroom-study
strategically placed between them.

Knowing that the rapidly developing physical strength and
marvellous health of her young pupils would accelerate their
sexual development, Madame always kept a tacit night
watch. Any traffic between the two dormitories would of
necessity have to pass her door – and, as one or two would-
be Romeos and Juliets had found out, Madame was a light
sleeper! Not that she was a prude. Indeed, as she had been
married herself at sixteen and had given birth to Anna at
seventeen, Madame, an incurable romantic, well knew the
pangs of adolescent love and turned a blind eye to it – but
not during term-time, and especially not at night, when her
exhausted pupils needed sleep to recuperate for their
ballet training on the morrow.

Her thoughts, however, were at that moment far removed
from her pupils' adolescent sex-problems, being totally
concentrated on how to woo the impending Inspector. As
she reached the bottom of the long flight of stairs, she walked
straight into the middle of a heated exchange in angry
Russian.

This fiery altercation had broken out, quite suddenly, in
the music room, where one of Madame's brothers-in-law,
Dmitri, had violently objected to his piano lesson being
interrupted by her other brother-in-law, Colonel Poliakoff,
who had arrived, suitably armed with paint and brushes, to
carry out some much-needed cosmetic decorating before the

Inspector arrived. A pot of emulsion had been spilled on the piano and this had caused Dmitri physically to attack his brother-in-law.

Like Igor Poliakoff, Dmitri Ulanov had once been in the service of the Czar, both as an artillery Captain and as a member of the 'Corps of Pages'. Now, with his short, stocky body quivering with righteous indignation, he had tried to push the tall, wiry Cossack out of the way. The Colonel had resisted valiantly and, locked in a close, panting embrace that had nothing of affection about it, they struggled out into the corridor, eloquently cursing each other in Russian.

The terrified Chinese girl music student had fled, crying for help, headlong into Madame's comforting arms as the two furious Russians tripped up and landed in a heap at her feet.

'Dmitri! Igor! Stop this foolishness at once – get up from floor!' commanded their sister-in-law.

Sheepishly, still breathing heavily, the two combatants rose to their feet and simultaneously broke into a voluble explanation of the incident. Colonel Poliakoff accused Dmitri of striking a superior officer, and Dmitri countered by accusing the Cossack of ruining the piano. It was then that during the tussle Dmitri had struck the Colonel with a wet paint rag, and his bristling whiskers still bore evidence of this insult. Failing a blow across the face with a pair of gloves, this had constituted an invitation to a duel, the choice of weapons resting with the insulted Cossack.

'Swords! Behind the stables – name your seconds!'

'Stop it, you imbeciles!' cried Madame. 'Your duel is not legal in England – not permitted!'

'Very well then, Natalia! I shall convene a court-martial of my regiment!'

'Court martial, fiddlesticks! Court would be biased – unacceptable! What chance would Dmitri, as artillery Captain, have against all-Cossack court? Not possible!'

'Then I will call upon ex-members of the Imperial Guard!'

'From where, Igor? Where are such people now?'

'General Felix Suliamov is commissionaire outside Troika Restaurant in Paris, Major Stephan Kucharski is taxi driver in Berlin, Colonel Pyotor Riabukianski is cleaner at Brighton Aquarium, Gregor – '

'Don't be ridiculous!' Madame's cutting tone interrupted the Colonel in full regimental spate. 'Apologize to each other immediately – or, Igor, we will lose grant for the school! Therefore no major redecoration! Dmitri, apologize – or no new piano!'

Faced with these dread alternatives, the angry ex-members of the Imperial Household grudgingly apologized and then, spurred on by Madame's predicament, hurried off to do something constructive against the common enemy in the person of the School Inspector.

Meanwhile Pamela had detailed several senior boys to work on the problem of the over-crowded dormitories, and now, together with Nat, was working out a rigged spelling test and a French conversation class. The latter would be the more impressive of the two supposedly unrehearsed displays of the Marashkova School's educational standard, because Anna, Madame and Nat all encouraged multi-lingual conversation during meal-times.

Anna went to see Madame just before midday to give her a quick rundown on the concert arrangements for the Hasting Concours that night. *The Spectre of the Rose* was being danced by Pamela and Dougal, and various extracts from ballets and divertissements had been rehearsed and polished close to perfection, as far as the young artistes were concerned. As Anna read through the names of the stars of the school, Madame's imagination pictured each dancer in turn, costumed and in character. Small, curly-haired Elizabeth from New Zealand, with her large dark eyes and her diminutive, sun-tanned body, as Coppelia; stately Julia, with her brilliant, ice-blue eyes and the long blond hair of her Viking ancestors, as the Snow Queen; Marianne,

Jeanne-Michelle, Toinette – and Illona, Madame's brilliant fourteen-year-old granddaughter, whose Slavic beauty was just beginning to blossom into flower. Then there was Dougal, and the surprising strength which gave his firm young body the resilience of a steel spring, perfectly fitting him for the title in *The Spectre of the Rose,* his splendid effortless elevation and apparent stop-motion pause in the middle of a grand jeté irresistibly reminding Madame of the great Nijinsky himself.

Each child, as Madame well knew, had chosen its own rôle and worked unceasingly at it throughout the year, attending classes held locally and in London during the holidays. Whether they came from Australia, Norway, Britain, Belgium, South Africa, Singapore, Japan, or any other part of the world, they were now Madame's girls – and boys – and she knew that they would shine that night.

The great secret of the Marashkova method of ballet was the 'line' of the dancers – that indefinable correct sense of proportion that gives an ethereal grace to athletic strength, something that only years of concentrated conditioning can give to the finished product: a properly trained dancer of the classical school of Russian ballet.

The Hour of the Inspection had arrived, and promptly at twelve noon an ancient but well-cared-for Morris saloon car pulled up outside the front entrance of the school. From it there stepped a neat, stout figure, which from the trilby hat set squarely on the greying sandy hair to the brogues on the feet, spelt out 'Civil Servant – Middle Grade' in Harris tweed letters. His leather-patched Norfolk jacket and well-pressed, worsted flannel trousers perfectly matched the personality – or rather non-personality – suggested by his pale, round face and steel-rimmed spectacles. These were set above an unimpressive potato of a nose and a thin mouth, topped by a close-clipped hint of a ginger moustache.

This was Mr Edgar Borwick, the dreaded scourge of fringe education, a small man – in both mind and body – who went round the county conscientiously dispelling any hopes of government grants that the unworthy might cherish in their optimistic hearts. He did not approve of unconventional private schools and maverick establishments such as the Marashkova School of Russian Ballet, Yoga and General Education. In fact, they were anathema to him. Thus, despite himself – for he was, oddly enough, a fair man – he had already mentally crossed off the school as being unsuitable for a grant. Nevertheless, he had to salve his conscience by properly inspecting it, so, brushing himself down and unrumpling his suit where it had creased during the journey, and carefully adjusting his expression to one of set purpose, he strode up to the door and pulled the bell handle beside it.

Before the bell had ceased jangling distantly, the door was opened by a pretty girl, dressed in the sober regulation school uniform which custom dictated and which Madame's pupils seldom wore.

'Can I help you?' asked the brightly-smiling, freckle-faced child.

'I am Mr Borwick,' stated the visitor in a tone which implied that this was the only credential he needed to enter the school.

'Do come in, please,' said the lovely young pupil, curtseying with accomplished grace. 'Perhaps you'd be so kind as to wait in the sitting-room.' She indicated the door of a room set to the left of the impressive entrance hall, and politely held it open for the School Inspector to enter.

'What do you wish to see Madame about?' she asked innocently as he seated himself.

The unexpected question came as a minor shock to the Inspector.

'I've come to inspect the school – I'm the School Inspector,' he declared somewhat foolishly in his confusion.

The small child smiled, carefully concealing her giggles, and left the School Inspector to cool his heels. A man with virtually no sense of humour, the Inspector mentally pulled up the socks of his composure and started looking round the large sitting-room. The walls were hung with faded photographs of great dancers, inscribed with expressions of gratitude to either Madame or her late husband. Supplying a touch of light relief to this rather formal scene were a number of wickedly funny cartoons of various famous ballet stars. Mr Borwick looked through his bifocals with disapproval at the mischievous caricatures so expertly drawn by the late Sergei Marashkov.

Suddenly the door was flung open and Madame swept in, followed by her staff – except for the headmaster, who, having been pumped full of black coffee by Nat, was now indisposed in the downstairs loo.

Before the Inspector could announce himself, Madame flourished the long-delayed official letter in front of him.

'Mistair Bor-wick,' she said firmly, pronouncing his name as though it were hyphenated, 'we have only just received word of your inspection this morning! Could your department not have telephoned me to say you were coming?'

This wasn't at all the sort of deferential greeting that the Inspector was accustomed to receiving, and he found himself losing some of his habitual composure.

'Possibly the postal strike is to blame,' he said defensively, in spite of himself.

'Possibly! Still, Mistair Bor-wick, since you are here perhaps is best you inspect! Come!'

'Thank you, Mrs – er,' the Inspector sought for the name.

'*Madame* Natalia Marashkova – I am Principal and Director of Marashkova School of Russian Ballet! Follow me!'

'Quite so, Madame Marashkova – thank you!'

The now flustered Inspector wished fervently that he hadn't come, and inwardly cursed the departmental delay that had already spoiled the whole tone of the inspection. Instead of being shown obsequiously around, he found himself following in the wake of this small, imperious woman, feeling uncomfortably close to inadequate.

Madame's arthritic limp in no way impeded her rapid progress down the hall towards the studio, from which the sound of a loud and methodically played piano could be heard, accompanied by that rhythmic swishing sound of massed ballet shoes which is the hallmark of a 'Class'.

In an effort to reinstate his damaged authority, the Inspector said, 'My name is spelled B-O-R-W-I-C-K, Madame, but it is pronounced *Borrick* –'

'So!' said Madame, turning with one hand on the handle of the double doors. 'Mistair *Borrrrick* –' she pronounced his name, deliberately rolling the 'r's', – 'this is ballet class in progress!'

She flung the doors open and the School Inspector followed her through them, to find himself confronted by two neat rows of dancers – boys on one side of the mirrored room and girls on the other – all dressed in their best black leotards and tights, with one arm firmly on the barres while their bodies assumed the disciplined pose of first position.

As the staff entered, Madame nodded imperceptibly and the senior boys and girls performed a beautifully executed mass bow and curtsey, as their sex dictated, before continuing with the class.

The Marashkova Ballet School being taken through an advanced class was something that even experienced dancers delighted in watching – the sheer grace of those perfectly developing young bodies performing the carefully graduated movements of ballet 'scales' was a spectacle to entrance the heart, and Mr Borwick was no exception. In spite of his deeply ingrained prejudice, the pompous little

man felt his soul give a gasp of pleasure at the sheer physical
beauty of the disciplined young dancers, and when the
display had obviously finished and the pupils had once
again bowed and curtseyed in unison, he just caught
himself in time as he was unconsciously about to applaud.

'You wish to inspect class?' Madame enquired sweetly.

'No! No! Indeed, Madame Marashkova – most impressive!' The Inspector saw his chance to regain the
initiative. 'Can we now see something of the academic
work of the school?' he said, in measured tones.

His hopes of an advantage were dashed as, with a curt
'Certainly,' Madame swept him along with her, while she
introduced her staff en route.

'My daughter Mrs Fenning – teaches Russian, German
and Geography. My son-in-law, Mistair Nathaniel Fenning
– teaches History, Mathematics and English. Headmaster –
Mistair MacClean – is today not well – influenza! However,
will meet you if possible. He is highly qualified academic –
M.A., B.A., B.Sc., – he deals with Higher Mathematics,
Physics and Chemistry. You will meet all staff at luncheon.
Ah! Here is combined French class with Poetry and
Literature. Enter!'

The Inspector walked into the airy classroom to face a
mass recitation of French poetry by a class of thirty pupils –
all of whom were standing on their heads, including the
teacher, who was actually Pamela, the head girl. As it is
extremely difficult to tell the age of someone who is upside
down without inverting yourself, Mr Borwick accepted her
in the rôle of teacher.

'Verlaine!' announced Madame.

'I beg your pardon?' stammered the now shaken Inspector.

'Verlaine!' repeated Madame patiently. 'French poetry
by great poet Verlaine.'

'Ah, quite so – of course! Most appropriate!' said the
Inspector hoarsely, wondering why he had used the word

'appropriate'. 'Isn't the class position a little – er – unusual, Madame?'

'Yoga exercise – reverses flow of blood – bringing better circulation to head! Naturally improves thinking and concentration, n'est-ce pas? C'est vrai! Regardez!'

Before Mr Borwick's goggling eyes Madame, without any preliminary warning, stood on her head, somehow managing at the same time to keep her dress perfectly adjusted in the interests of propriety. From her now inverted position she addressed the class.

'Mes enfants! Permettez-moi de vous présenter Monsieur l'Inspecteur des Ecoles!'

A chorus of well-rehearsed 'Bonjour, Monsieur, soyez le bienvenu,' issued from the inverted class.

'Bonjour!' the flummoxed Inspector eventually managed to stutter.

'Continuez, mes enfants!' said Madame, as she effortlessly regained her feet. 'You wish to address class, Mistair Borrick?' she enquired.

'No, thank you – most impressive – er, I don't think I've ever seen that method of teaching employed before, Madame.'

Madame ruthlessly pressed home her obvious advantage. 'Regretfully, Mistair Borrick, you have come at the moment when you catch the school unawares. We could – had your Department given us due warning – have presented you with more interesting programme. However, perhaps before inspecting school buildings you will have luncheon? Good. This way, Mistair Borrick!'

It was a measure of how strong a psychological advantage Madame Marashkova had already gained over the normally self-assured School Inspector that he accepted her invitation without demur, and followed her meekly to the dining-room, which had been skilfully converted from the building's original cellars. This clever piece of architectural adaptation was the work of Madame's nephew, Andrei de

Waldenheim, who had just finished at university and was
working as a draughtsman for a local builder, whose
daughter, it goes without saying, was a pupil at the Marashkova School.

This very bright young man was gifted with a cheerful
disposition, a great deal of Russian charm, and could, enter-
tainingly and with apparent authority, talk the hind leg off
a donkey – or for that matter a School Inspector. Madame
was keeping her nephew in reserve; as the French generals
call it, the '*masse de manoeuvre*', and now brought up her
reinforcements by placing Andrei next to the School Inspector, where he could be most effective.

Just before grace, they were joined at the top table by
Babushka and the headmaster, who looked pale and unwell,
thus giving confirmation of Madame's earlier explanation
of his absence, and after the first course, appropriately of
Scotch broth, he excused himself and hastily retired from
the scene.

'Poor man,' cooed Madame sympathetically. 'He has been
working too hard to bring pupils up to "A" levels – no
resistance to influenza – should practise yoga more frequently!'

The Inspector was duly impressed by the general
excellence of the food and accepted, unwisely and very
much against his normal practice, a glass of claret, and then,
fascinated by Andrei's fluent description of the history of
the school buildings, most of which had little foundation in
fact, he accepted another.

During the course of the lunch, the pupils were busy
chattering away in their several languages, while Madame
and her staff deliberately fluctuated between French,
German and, for once, Russian. By now, the Inspector was
becoming putty in Madame's expressive hands, for Natalia
Marashkova could, when she wanted to, charm the birds
from the trees.

The whole ambience of the school and the heady presence

of Madame's unusual family, together with a third glass of excellent Bordeaux, had reached some hither-to hidden chord in the Inspector's soul and gently plucked it. Quite suddenly, over coffee, he confided, 'I used to dance a bit myself, Madame.' His round, slightly flushed face glowed at the memory. 'When I was in the R.A.F. – at the Hammersmith Palais de Danse – when I was on leave. That's where I met Gladys – Mrs Borwick. Of course, it was only ballroom dancing, but I enjoyed it. I haven't danced for years!' The little man finished regretfully, and Madame instantly saw a further chink in her opponent's armour, and lunged neatly below his lowered guard.

'So, Mistair Borrick – you dance! You do not surprise me. See! You are built like dancer,' here Madame expertly ran seductive fingers over the Inspector's arm. 'You are in very good condition for a mature man – good biceps strong wrists – you practise yoga perhaps?'

Considerably flattered, the 'Terror of the Private Schools' blushed until his sandy complexion shone with a healthy pink.

'Well, I do play bowls a bit – that's not an old man's game by any means, even though a lot of people think it is!'

'You should do ballet exercises at the barre, Mistair Borrick. Many local parents, who are busy professional people like yourself, come to my special evening classes combining yoga and ballet. Is very good for tired business people exhausted from too much sitting down!'

Deep within Mr Borwick's totally seduced mind the last despairing cry of his vocation impinged on his conciousness.

'Very kind of you to offer, Madame. Now, if we could continue the inspection, I should like to see the dormitories.'

'Naturally, Mistair Borrick,' nodded the great ballet teacher, half in assent to the Inspector's request and half in acknowledgement of Nat's signal that these rooms were cleared for action.

'You must excuse me, however. I have to get my pupils ready for the Concours at Hastings tonight. Their bus leaves at three.' She held out an elegant hand, which the Inspector nearly kissed, but at the last moment, Madame lowered her fingers and perfunctorily shook hands. 'My son-in-law and my nephew Andrei de Waldenheim will escort you.'

With that, Madame spun nimbly on her heel and strode purposefully past the grand staircase and vanished out of sight down the corridor, while Nat and Andrei shepherded the Inspector upstairs to where the dormitories were awaiting inspection.

When he finally gazed at the lines of well-spaced, perfectly made beds, Mr Borwick's eyes glowed with pleasure. He could not have guessed that two rooms ahead of his tour of inspection a third one was packed tight with the extra bunks and bedding that had been hastily tranferred from the one in which he was standing.

'Excellent!' he said, marking a tick against the appropriate section of the pro forma which he held clipped to a board. 'Very neatly and – er – correctly – er – '

'Space allocated?' suggested Andrei smoothly. 'All our dormitories are carefully pupil-orientated – space wise, that is. 'Of course,' he continued, 'we use cheerful chintzes and plain but non-institutional furniture – it gives a more home-ly atmosphere to the dormitories. Many of our young boarders are first-time-away-from-home children as well as coming from overseas.'

'So I noticed! Excellent idea! I'm most impressed.'

Steered neatly past the third dormitory, which was now jammed to the ceiling with all the unwanted bric-à-brac, the Inspector allowed himself to be guided through an equally cursory inspection of the girls' dormitories.

'Alles in Ordnung!' whispered Nat to his wife as they met briefly in the hall.

At that precise moment Mr Borwick, quite innocently, dropped a bombshell: 'I must, of course, just see the fire-escape,' he announced, smiling benignly. 'That is vital.'

Andrei felt as if he had been kicked in the stomach by a Cossack pony, but managed to say: 'Naturally! As you so rightly say – the fire escape is a vitally important part of the fabric of the school. This way, please!'

While he led the School Inspector on the most circuitous route he could think of, stopping to point out anything that might conceivably be of the slightest architectural interest, Nat excused himself and pelted up towards the flat roof, gathering up six of the strongest lads on the way.

Actually the school had perfectly adequate fire precautions in the shape of extinguishers, red-painted buckets filled with sand and water, and even rolled-up asbestos blankets and, with their high standard of physical fitness and acrobatic ability, the pupils, who all slept on the first floor, could easily have made their escape – if the need had ever arisen. Moreover, under the resourceful and calm command of Madame, Nat, Anna and Andrei, there would be no panic, and the only risk would be to the headmaster, who might well be too far gone in his cups to hear the alarm. Nevertheless, Andrei knew that the one structural alteration that needed immediate attention, once funds became available, was the school fire escape.

Luckily Anna had made plans for just such an emergency as this unexpected request for a fire drill inspection, and gave Andrei a reassuring wave with her handkerchief from a first floor window on the escape route.

'Looks substantial enough!' said Mr Borwick as they arrived at the foot of the antique metal construction.

'And so it is!' agreed Andrei, taking the Inspector's arm to lead him away. 'They don't build them like that nowadays!'

'I must just test it, however,' said the conscientious Mr Borwick, firmly grasping the black metal ladder and shaking it.

It moved visibly, but held firm, Andrei covering its

swaying with a swift: 'We allow a certain flexibility – we have very high winds here! Too rigid a structure would break up unless it could, as it were, bend slightly with the wind!'

'Quite so,' agreed Mr Borwick, placing a cautious foot on the bottom rung, and proceeding to climb the swaying ladder.

Andrei had done his best and now stood, holding on as hard as he could without seeming to, smiling confidently while his heart skipped a few beats. He need not have worried, for, as the Inspector mounted high enough to come level with the girls' dormitory, Anna played her trump card.

As Mr Borwick's face appeared outside the open window, three scantily-clad senior girls, their hands clasped in virgin modesty over their budding breasts, gave a simultaneous and resounding shriek, nearly causing the horrified Inspector to lose his balance. Mumbling profuse apologies, he hastily retreated down the shaking iron ladder, and only Andrei's ready hands saved him from a nasty tumble at the bottom.

'Yes, it's fine!' he gasped out. 'Thank you for showing me – I see your point about the high winds. Good idea! Must make a note of that.'

As he mopped his damply disturbed brow, he little guessed at the six boys on the roof grimly hanging on to the end of the fire escape, ably assisted by Nat, acting as anchorman, maintaining a living, bionic fastening to the whole structure.

Mr Borwick was now convinced that Madame Marashkova ran a tight ship – unconventional certainly !– but with obviously intelligent and well-behaved pupils, and with a strong regard for the stringent requirements of the Education Act. Unaware that he had been spared an introduction to Professor Karma (he was enjoying the afternoon sun on a bed of nails at the far end of the garden), and those other

members of Madame's entourage who did not bear close
inspection – including one or two injured Cossacks and a
distant cousin who suffered from a paranoiac fear of the
K.G.B. and spent most of his time locked in the attic, Mr
Borwick was completely satisfied with his inspection.

Madame had neatly engineered an exciting 'Farewell and
God-speed' ceremony for the departing bus-load of seniors,
each of whom bowed or curtseyed to the School Inspector
in the character that he or she was to dance that evening,
while Madame rattled off the roll-call: 'Julia – Snow Queen!
Elizabeth – Coppelia! Pamela – Sleeping Beauty! Illona –
Scheherezade! Toinette – Giselle! Dougal – Spectre of the
Rose! Herman – Prince! Robert – Wicked Wizard! Wong
– Slave!' and so on.

As the long line of talented youngsters passed before him
with their excited faces full of anticipation and confidence,
the final change was wrought in the School Inspector's
whirling senses, and he found himself happily bowing back
to this stream of eager disciples of the dance.

That was the phrase that tripped through Mr Borwick's
mind, as he waved as enthusiastically as the Marashkova
school staff, until the bus passed out of sight through the
gates.

'Well, Mistair Borrick?' said Madame, smiling quizzically
at his unaccustomedly happy face. 'You will stay for tea?
Yes?'

'I would very much like to – but I have to get back to
Maidstone.' The School Inspector's voice held genuine
regret. 'But – before I go – may I have a word with you –
er – in private?'

A feeling of cold dread touched the hearts of Anna and
Nat, while Andrei shuffled uncomfortably behind them.
Madame, however, showed not a tremor of emotion as
she gravely inclined her small, bird-like head, and led the
somewhat embarrassed Inspector into the staff common-
room.

As she closed the door behind them, Natalia Marashkova offered up a silent prayer – partly to God and partly to
the shade of her discarnate husband.

'So, Mistair Borrick?' she gently queried, waiting
fatalistically for his final verdict.

'Madame – I don't quite know how to put this to you.'
His small, stocky frame wriggled uncomfortably before
her, reminding Madame more of a recalcitrant pupil than
the awesome agent of officialdom.

'Please, feel free, Mistair Borrick.' Her quiet dignity had
all the controlled discipline of an *aristo* on her way, in the
tumbril, to the guillotine.

'Very well, Madame Marashkova.' The School Inspector
cleared his throat, and plunged straight in. 'I have a
problem! My daughter Mavis – a nice girl and quite
talented, but not, you understand, gifted academically –
she's more – well – artistic! Unfortunately she is not happy
at her present educational establishment – an excellent
school, but somehow, for a sensitive child like Mavis, it's
– well! – a bit too formal. Inflexible, one might say. I was
wondering if you could see your way to taking her? Of
course, I realize that you must have a substantial waiting-
list, but I would be most grateful if you – er . . .'

The rest of his words were lost to Madame. The warm
glow of the westering summer sun poured in through the
windows, filling the room with burnished bronze light,
and Natalia Marashkova felt the strong arms and laughing
presence of her beloved husband as his joyous spirit embraced her, making her soul silently cry out:

'We've won, Sergei! My darling – we've won!'

Heritage

'YOU HAVE JUST COST this newspaper twenty thousand
pounds in legal expenses and, as far as I am concerned, that
automatically fires you – as from now!'

William Barraclough glared over his old fashioned half-
moon glasses at his sports reporter, Mike Moloney. 'You
would be on your way to Accounts to collect severance
pay but for one factor in your favour – which, frankly, I
hate to admit – Moloney, you are a bloody good reporter!'

The object of this tirade looked quizzically at his editor,
surprised at his use of the word 'bloody', because 'Old
Bill' Barraclough was never known to swear even mildly –
a trait which was quite contrary to the popular conception
of the hard-drinking, hard-swearing newspaper man.

'Old Bill' paused to catch his venomous breath and then
continued his monologue: 'Your last two years, as our top
sports leader writer, have earned this newspaper an enor-
mously increased following, and your efforts have been
largely instrumental in pulling it out of the red. But this
last piece of yours, on graft in contemporary soccer, was ill

considered, ill advised and, in the expert opinion of our
legal advisers, ill timed. It was also so well written that its
impact was tremendous – and the same can be said for the
follow-up story. But, good as it was, your story presented
this newspaper with a potentially ruinous lawsuit which,
by settling out of court and profusely apologizing, we have
managed to avoid by the skin of our dentures. However!'
The editor leaned forward, his small, hunched body seeming to uncoil like a striking snake, as he stared mesmerically
at his erring scribe. 'I am not going to fire you – at least,
not yet. You are going to be punished in a different and,
much as I loathe the adjective, meaningful way. By using
that word in its correct context, I hope to convey to you
the harsh fact that a lesson has got to be learnt and that the
only way for you to learn it is by experience. That lesson,
Moloney, is to keep that raging Irish temper of yours under
strict control – at least in print! So I am putting your undoubt-
ed talents to work in the one section of this newspaper where
you can say what you think and no one is going to sue us
because of it. I refer, Moloney, to the Arts section!'

The wiry, well-built frame of the Irishman suddenly
quivered with fury and his tousled dark-red hair seemed to
rustle with righteous indignation as he banged the editor's
desk with a protesting fist.

'Jesus Christ – I hate the bloody theatre! Films bore the
balls off me – and I'll be buggered in Spades if I'll take this
from you, you ungrateful bastard!'

'May I remind you, Moloney,' said 'Old Bill' sweetly,
apparently unmoved by the outburst, 'that you happen to
have a contract with this newspaper for the next two years
– and one small clause in it states . . .' Here the editor
picked up a document from a slim file in front of him, and
slowly and deliberately read out: ' *"The party of the second
part* – that's you, Moloney – *shall undertake such assignments
as the party of the first part* – that's the newspaper and by
inference me, its editor – *shall deem necessary provided that no*

unreasonably dangerous circumstances, etc., etc." – well, that's the part which applies to war correspondents –'

'That I'll take!' Moloney butted in furiously. 'Send me anywhere you like – I'll cover any war, revolution, civil disturbance, uprising, crazy outbreaks of mindless terrorism or what-bloody-have-you, but Sweet Jesus! Not the stinking Arts page!'

Mike Moloney in full cry epitomized the larger-than-life image of a Fleet Street reporter so beloved by film scenario writers. His editor, however, remained imperturbable in the face of his desperate plea.

'You will take this assignment forthwith, and you will deposit on my desk, by next Friday morning, the first-fruits of your new artistic labours, the relevant details of which you will find in this box file –' He pushed a well-filled cardboard container across the desk so that it slid neatly into Moloney's lap. The reporter automatically caught it with the neat, fast reaction that had once made him a fine wicket-keeper for England.

'Read the title!' hissed his tormentor.

Moloney, still fuming with now inarticulate rage, focused his eyes on the file's cover label and almost spat out the words: ' "Masterpiece or Forgery?" So what? What the hell can I write about this sort of high falutin' crap? God in heaven! What kind of story-line's that? What does it amount to?'

The wizened little editor stopped the Irishman's tirade with three words.

'One Million Pounds!'

Moloney abruptly closed his mouth and started to listen.

'Ah!' purred 'Old Bill'. 'I thought that might just spark off a glimmer of interest in that mercenary soul of yours. Now follow me carefully, Mike!'

The reporter noted the sudden change in his editor's mode of address. So! It was back to Christian names!

'This story could well be a potential prize winner, if you

can crack it wide open, and it's the sort of assignment that your average so-called art-expert-cum-critic could neither adequately investigate nor properly handle, even if, somehow, he managed to ferret out the truth. Your starting point is that in the last two years two sketches by an old master have suddenly come on to the art market at auction and each of them has netted half a million pounds sterling!'

'Sketches?' queried Moloney, his journalistic instincts finding a rapidly growing interest in the assignment. 'Not finished paintings? Just sketches?'

'Sketches!' repeated the editor with smug satisfaction, now certain that he had hooked his catch. 'Drawings and explanatory notes, by the hand of the one old master whose work commands at least a half a million pounds a page – Leonardo da Vinci. Shall I go on?'

The question was superfluous as Moloney rose from his chair with the contents of the box file clutched in both hands.

'Holy Mother of God,' he breathed reverently. 'What a story!'

He made for the door of the editor's suite, only pausing as Barraclough's voice brought him back to the unanswered question.

'What about it, Mike?'

The Irishman half turned, his hand already on the door knob. He grinned with a freckled warmth that spelt out Gaelic Charm in every feature of his handsome face and very deliberately said:

'On your desk – Friday!'

The bleak Monday morning seemed filled with spring sunshine, as Moloney set out for a self-congratulatory lunch at The Cheshire Cheese – that tourist-oriented but still professionally patronized seventeenth-century pub, just off the bustle of Fleet Street. The Irishman's purpose was two-fold. He felt that he deserved to treat himself to a small celebration in the form of a delicious home-made steak and mushroom pie, washed down with a couple of pints of draught Guinness; in addition, he knew that he would find some invaluable preliminary guidance in his new assignment if a certain friend of his was ensconced, as usual, in his favourite corner of the bar.

His hoped-for informant was already there, in full flight of rhetorical fancy, as he harangued a fascinated colleague.

'So, my dear boy, I literally cut the play to ribbons – like sliced Mortadella – especially the third act, which, let me tell you, was nothing but an inept pastiche of Molière – with overtones of Shaw – out of Coward by John Osborne! A miserable fake pedigree, you'll agree when you go to see it – that is, of course, providing that it is still on by the end of its fortnight's mandatory Equity-guaranteed run! It's a pig, dear boy – a hundred percent non-Danish home grown bore!'

'Percy!' interrupted Moloney, tapping the flamboyant speaker on the shoulder: 'I need your advice.'

Percy Watkins-Bradshaw stopped in mid bon mot and surveyed the Irishman. It was one of Percy's odd traits that he surveyed rather than just looked at people.

'Laddie!' he said finally. 'What on God's little green earth would cause the Emerald Isle's scourge of bent sportsmanship to seek words with the humble literate soul of yours truly?'

'I'll buy you lunch!'

Percy was, for a brief moment, bereft of words. 'Lunch?' he repeated faintly, like a Regency dandy challenged to a sudden duel: 'Did you say lunch? A la carte lunch? With a decent claret?' Here his voice became a shade stronger, as he recovered from his apparent attack of the vapours. 'Like a vintage Margaux?' By this time his fine baritone voice had regained its normal rounded vigour. 'In the name of all that's reviewable – why? What for?'

Moloney smiled that partly carefully cultivated, partly quite natural, devastating smile of his that had been the downfall of a number of very attractive women.

'Only you can help me, Percy,' he said, quite sincerely, believing it, at that stage of the proceedings, to be the case.

The art, literary, stage and film critic bowed and waved a languid hand in assent.

'What can I say? Except that the generosity of your expense account is more than kind. Lead on, dear boy!'

Mike knew that behind his front of effete cynicism, Percy Watkins-Bradshaw hid a keen, well-honed mind and knew and cared about everything that was genuinely best in the Arts. His flat refusal to take over the job of television columnist when the position had become vacant reflected his total integrity – especially as the salary involved had been double his present one.

Once seated on one of the high-backed dark oak benches which gave The Cheshire Cheese part of its unique ambience, the process of carefully ordering and enjoying the quite splendid, simply-cooked English traditional fare was a matter of delightful routine. The fine old claret, at precisely the right temperature and in just the right quantity, eased down the generous portions of succulent smoked trout, steak and kidney pie, new potatoes and fresh garden peas, followed by a refreshing raspberry syllabub and rounded off, in truly Dickensian style, with incomparable English white Stilton. It now needed only an ample supply of excellent vintage port to complete its perfect gastronomic balance. As they finished their third glass Watkins-Bradshaw spoke:

'So it's good-bye sports page and hail to thee, Blithe Spirit of the Arts – Christ, what a switch! No critical literary lion thou, Michael. Just like that cunning old bastard to put you on to the Leonardo sketches. I wondered what he would do with you, when the groaning board thirsted after your Irish blood, old son! Investigative journalism in the Arts, eh? That'll set the marmalade cat among the auction room doves and no mistake!'

'All right, Percy,' Mike said. 'Come clean – what do you really know about the Leonardo sketches? Are they or aren't they genuine?'

The elegant Arts correspondent suddenly laughed, with a resounding gusto that momentarily turned the heads of the other diners and belied the languid image which he so carefully used to front his unfashionable zest for life.

'God dammit, Mike, I'm not a bloody art expert. I don't know if they're the real McCoy or not! Look how long it took the professionals to spot that Dutchman, Van Meegeren and his faked Vermeers. And what about Tom Keating's pastiches of Samuel Palmer's watercolours? They had a lot of experts hiding their red faces in shame. Even the Victoria and Albert Museum has had to re-attribute a number of their Constables to the credit of his son and other members of the Dedham Vale Constabulary. After all, the provenance of a picture lies in its history – in how many experts, for how long, have accepted the work as genuinely being by the hand of the artist.

'In the case of these two Leonardo sketches – or as they were improperly called, cartoons – well, laddie, they only appeared on the art market some two years ago. All I can tell you is that they caused a fine old furore. Not among the public for whom it was, at best, a nine-day wonder – that is if good old Joe Public even noticed their existence. But, oh mate, the fluttering in the dovecotes of the art world sounded more like the beating of avenging angels' wings when – *after* the sales – some experts suddenly failed to agree as to their authenticity.'

'So much I gathered, Percy,' said Moloney impatiently. 'But surely there must be conclusive tests and highly specialized techniques for establishing the validity of this sort of thing?'

'Myriad ones, Michael, me broth of a boyo,' replied Percy, reverting to his corny public character image. 'Every expert has his own particular penchant for some obscure treatise on ancient paper fibres, or the chemical composition of archaic inks and hand ground paint pigments; but even with x-rays of the paintings, canvasses and panel backings of the old masters, no two experts seem able to agree on anything, beyond the authenticity and probable age of the ingredients. Certainly never on the artist! So then it's up to the consensus of informed opinion to influence the artistic decision, and it needs a final attribution by some important gallery or museum, or even top expert opinion in the sales room, before that particular work gets the seal of genuine approval.

'In the case of these Leonardo sketches, nobody seems eager now to take the responsibility of a final definitive attribution – and that after the drawings have changed hands at a nice round half a million each. Either the sketches are worth every penny – supposing that you can put a price on the work of a great master – or they are extremely clever fakes and worth, at the most, a couple of thousand for their curiosity value! Frankly, Mike, only Leonardo himself knows the truth – so what's going to be your angle, sonny boy?'

Moloney smiled enigmatically. 'That's my secret,' he said. 'My secret and my lunch. Thanks a million, Percy, for the information about the sketches. Let's see that's half a million thanks each sketch!'

'My gastronomic pleasure,' rumbled Percy contentedly.

Moloney's next stop was at one of London's most celebrated auction houses. A self-assured, rapier-thin young man, of obvious breeding and consummate ability, answered his queries with that subtle mixture of tolerance, civility and a slight air of patronage which is the hallmark of an art auction expert. Yes, he agreed, there was a small amount of doubt regarding the authenticity of the Leonardo sketches – but then again, the reservations of some of the experts arose from the odd fact that two such outstanding works of world-wide importance should have remained undiscovered for so long.

Nevertheless, he continued, as far as the scientific tests were concerned both sketches, on identical paper, had emerged vindicated to the last fibre of paper and the last bold line of ancient ink.

Every acknowledged scholar of the great Leonardo da Vinci – including a hand-writing expert – had agreed that the sketches were indistinguishable from authenticated examples of the master's method, style and unapproachable skill. The only snag was, of course, the coincidence factor and, in the case of both sketches, the subject matter, for the precognitive inventive genius of the mind that had already drawn tanks, flying machines, submarines and numerous other twentieth-century inventions, had now surpassed itself with drawings of a three-stage rocket and what looked suspiciously like a hovercraft. The two pages of beautifully-executed pen and ink sketches also included an ingenious machine gun with modern-style brass cartridges, an improved helicopter and a complete frogman's outfit in waterproofed leather, which almost exactly resembled the Cousteau/Gagnan equipment.

'Of course,' the bright young art-expert summed up, 'the drawings, like all Leonardo's work in this genre, show a primitive version of each artifact rather than a clearly-defined working drawing – but then, after all, he didn't possess the actual machines to copy from. Nevertheless, the principles are clearly shown and, to me, they are one more confirmation of Leonardo's genius.'

At the Courtauld Institute, Moloney found even more expert guidance from the cleaning and restoration authorities, who had examined the sketches by every means available.

'We used x-ray analysis, chemical analysis, thermo-luminescence and infra-red scanning techniques and, as far as the materials are concerned, we are quite satisfied as to their authenticity. We also understand that Colin Bloy of Johnson & Bloy's Inks has examined samples of the medium used and pronounced it quite genuine – and as he is a leading world expert on this subject we would accept his judgment.

'The paper has been thoroughly examined and tested and as for the actual work itself – we are confident, that it is the hand of the master! Even that splendid eccentric scholar, the late lamented Dr Henry 'Franz' Pultizer who claimed, with good reasons, to possess an original Leonardo painting of the Mona Lisa was quite certain that the hand was that of Leonardo da Vinci.

'However, we come up against the same old stumbling-block to credibility – no previous provenance exists, or has been hinted at which would explain the sudden appearance of both sketches and their presence on the art market.'

'Who did the drawings belong to?' asked Moloney. 'Surely there must be a record of the last owner, before the sketches appeared at auction?'

'Only the auction house could give you that information,' replied the expert with finality.

Barraclough himself made the necessary enquiries using his name and influence to circumvent the usually impenetrable barrier of secrecy that surrounds such information. His assurance of discretion was accepted and, after a couple of intercontinental telephone calls, a name was discreetly passed, with the owner's permission, via Barraclough to the impatient Moloney.

On Friday the Irishman, as promised, deposited the first article on his delighted editor's desk, and Barraclough's beaming smile contrasted completely with their earlier meeting.

'It means catching the Air France plane to Charles de Gaulle Airport before midday tomorrow. Full expenses, Mike, and this will please you! – you will be met by a quite delightful representative of ours in Paris!'

Moloney caught the eleven o'clock airbus and some forty minutes later was coming in to land at that most advanced of all contemporary air terminals. Minutes after the engines were switched off, the Irishman was gliding up one of the Plexiglass-tube-enclosed escalators, feeling a little like neatly-packaged meat, as he was processed through Customs and Immigration with commendable speed.

Barraclough's prediction, as usual, proved to be correct and Moloney found himself ten minutes later racing down the autoroute into Paris, in a chauffeur-drive Citroen, while beside him the lusciously French presence of Mademoiselle Elaine Bouvry-Salignac made him wish he had more time to enjoy her company. A lovely, self-possessed young woman, Elaine was not only a delight to the eye, in her suède trench coat with its inimitable French chic, she was also a product of the Beaux Arts and the Sorbonne and held two degrees – one in physics and the other in literature.

Moloney grinned appreciatively at her and quickly surmised that she would be the most perfect dinner and after-dinner companion since Gaelic coffee. His deceptively lazy 'bedroom eyes' had already taken in every detail of her femininity during the ponderous progress of the *belle époque* elevator that had lifted them, in close proximity, to the third floor of the elegant Hotel Bristol on the Faubourg St Honoré, which was to be his headquarters.

When the two were finally left alone by the under-manager in the charming suite thoughtfully provided by Barraclough, it would not have been difficult for Moloney to imagine that they were a honeymoon couple about to enjoy the consummation of a perfect marriage. His mood communicated itself to his companion, who smiled warmly as she said, 'The Bristol has that effect on most people! One feels that the hotel was created to be enjoyed by young lovers – or am I mistaking that look in your blue Irish eyes?'

Moloney laughed at being caught out in his thoughts so soon. 'Dear God! Mademoiselle, does it show that much?'

'No! But I was once engaged to an Irishman, and I detected the same reaction to the ambience of this place!'

'He was a lucky man, Mademoiselle.'

'Please call me Elaine!'

'Then it's Mike – Elaine.'

'I prefer Michael. It is such a beautiful name,' said the unruffled and delectable French girl as she gently and naturally flirted with her attractive colleague.

'Was he a journalist?' continued Moloney, probing for more information.

'A writer! He loved fast cars and Scotch whisky – and women. He was killed with one of the latter while driving one of the former – being full of his other love at the time! I'm sorry – I'm boring you!'

'Not at all, Elaine! *I'm* sorry,' the Irishman replied gently, now knowing for certain that the two of them would, at some future time, completely enjoy each other. But not now!

'So, Michael! I have already made the preliminary research for you.'

'Excellent! Where do we go from here?'

'Not very far – just down the Faubourg St Honoré. You know Paris well?'

'Not really. Only as a tourist.'

'Then you will already know that the Faubourg has some of the most chic shops in Paris including, of course, some small and very expensive galleries. It is to one of these that we go next! The owner's name is Chantal Verlaine – a wealthy widow, who inherited her late husband's excellent and well-respected art dealing business. We have an appointment with her in thirty minutes.'

'What's her exact connection with the sketches?'

'I don't know. Only that Monsieur Barraclough telephoned me with the information that the Verlaine Gallery had been the only provenance, so far, in the handling of the sale of the Leonardo sketches.'

'Well done, darlin' – fine! We'll soon get the information we want.'

Elaine rose to her small, elegantly-shod feet and they were soon on their way to keep their appointment. After the inevitable round of formal hand-shaking, Moloney was left alone with another chic, charmingly feminine French businesswoman – in this case somewhat older with a small 'tuck' from an expert plastic surgeon that gave her a slightly fragile loveliness, in contrast to the healthy glow of youth enjoyed by the younger Elaine. Moloney launched straight into his enquiries.

'Can you tell me how the Leonardo sketches came into your possession, Madame?'

'Certainly. There is nothing in the least shady in the affair. The sketches, about which I understand there are now some ridiculous doubts, are quite genuine and came into our hands through an old friend, Monsieur Sergei Lubovitch, a White Russian émigré friend of my late husband. They were in the Resistance together, you understand? Bon!'

The elegant Madame Verlaine obviously had nothing to hide behind her beautiful professional smile, which would have made a less experienced and confident man than Moloney feel gauche and inept.

'And this Russian gentleman owned the sketches?'

'Not in the strict sense, no! He acted as an *entrepreneur*! I don't know the word in English, Monsieur.'

'Entrepreneur will do just fine, Madame!'

'Bon! The whole business was so bizarre. My friend Monsieur Lubovitch was thoroughly trustworthy and had brought to us – sadly for him – several charming pieces which he had taken out from Russia. My husband had purchased them or acted as the agent in selling them.'

'Then the Leonardos came from Russia?'

'No! The strange part of the story is how they came into Sergei's possession. It was through a friend of his in Florence!'

'An Italian dealer or collector?'

'*Pas du tout*! It was from another war comrade, an Englishman, but he was living in Florence – at least he was when he wrote to Sergei saying that he was coming with the drawings.'

'This Englishman must have had complete confidence in your Russian friend, Madame, to entrust such treasures to him.'

'Indeed yes! Apparently during the war Sergei had saved the Englishman's life, when their Resistance cell – a Maquis organization – had been betrayed by one of their number. This Englishman, who lived in Florence, gave Sergei the drawings and he brought them to me. He told me that his friend wished him to sell them for him – apparently his friend was in delicate health and preferred to remain in the background.'

'Can I speak to Monsieur Lubovitch?' asked the Irishman eagerly.

'Tragically, no! The exciting news that the sketches were genuine – as the Englishman suspected – and the commission which we were able to pay Sergei from the eventual sale in London – all this brought on a fatal heart attack. Just as all his troubles seemed to be over!'

Well, they're certainly over now, thought Moloney to himself, as he considered his next move. Then, his mind made up, he took the plunge.

'The Englishman in Florence – can I contact him?'

'Again, Monsieur Moloney, I can only give you the address where he was last known to be living. Apparently he only went to Florence from time to time, but Sergei's sister knows his last address.'

A short telephone call to the late Sergei Lubovitch's
sister elicited the required information, and Moloney
scribbled down 'Macmillan, c/o Pensione Armadeo, Via
Zenobia, Firenze' on the back of one of Madame Verlaine's
elegant business cards.

Though Moloney and Elaine Bouvry-Salignac would
have been delighted to explore further their mutual attrac-
tion, they both had enough professional integrity to
postpone any dalliance, recognizing the necessity of
Moloney's following up the lead as soon as possible. A
further phone call to Barraclough clinched the matter and
Moloney lifted off from the runway at Charles de Gaulle
Airport at 20.00 hours exactly, en route for Florence, with
the memory of the soft eager warmth of Elaine's lips and a
strong feeling of frustration to remind him of an all too
short half-hour alone with her. Next time! he mused
comfortingly to himself – and please God – make it
soon!

The plane landed at Leonardo da Vinci Airport in Rome,
the coincidence giving Moloney a strange prophetic feeling
of optimism. Here he was met by the Rome correspondent
of his newspaper, Vincenzo Renaldo, a tall, wirily-built
Italian with grey curly hair, who had been in the Partigiani
as a young boy and had kept himself in trim by not falling
into the trap of too much pasta and good wine.

As they drove to Florence Renaldo gave Moloney as
much information as he could, culled from the enquiries he
had made regarding the Pensione Armadeo following his
long telephone conversation with Barraclough in London.

The facts were simple enough. The Pensione Armadeo
was owned, not too surprisingly, by a Signor Giulio
Armadeo, a respected Florentine hotelier of impeccable
references, and indeed an Englishman, named Dr Edward
Macmillan, had stayed there every summer at around the
same time for a number of years, each visit lasting approximately four weeks with the exception of one visit, a couple

of years before, when he had been unfortunate enough to catch double pneumonia, and had been nursed by the Armadeo ménage.

When Moloney and his voluble Rome-born companion arrived at the Pensione, Signor Armadeo confirmed the details, speaking in a delightful mixture of Florentine dialect and American English, which entranced Moloney's ear, as much as its content interested him.

'Sure! Il Dottore Macmillan – he come here every summer – nice man – clean living man – intelligente man with crazy pastimes – love to dig – always he dig – *corpo di Bacco*! How he love to dig around the old monastery ruin where he say he look for – how is it in English? Si! Proof of his big hero – Leonardo da Vinci. Always he looking for proof that one time Leonardo he live in the monastery! Si! Si! Il Dottore Macmillan – he crazy about Leonardo!'

He was modest to a degree about having nursed the ailing doctor back to health. 'He very good patient – you say? No! Si! Si! Nice man – gentleman – il dottore – very sick – but he pull through – Dottore Angelo di Calferta he say il Dottore Macmillan very lucky man to make it – but better he stay here – after so many visits where he comfortable and he can have my Gina's good minestrone. Not to go to hospital where the food she is terrible! No!'

Moloney asked Signor Armadeo the 64,000 dollar question – could he give them any information as to the good doctor's whereabouts at present? And the obliging Florentine rummaged in his files, until he triumphantly emerged with Dr Macmillan's last known address in England – at Bromley in Kent.

Having acquired the interesting information that the elusive doctor was an amateur archaeologist as well as a great admirer of Leonardo da Vinci, Moloney thanked the delightful Armadeo family for all their help, drove at breakneck speed to Rome, where he telephoned Barraclough to tell him the results of his visit to Florence, and caught the next plane for London – regretfully having to by-pass Paris and the delights of Elaine Bouvry-Salignac.

Once in London Moloney telephoned Barraclough's home immediately to get any information which might have arisen from his earlier phone call at Rome Airport, when he had passed on the details provided by Signor Armadeo.

Already, as Moloney had guessed, Barraclough's staff – namely his jewel of a private secretary, Miss Jill Carlsen – had come up with quite a lot of background information on Dr Edward Macmillan, M.B. (Ph.D. Psychology) and various other highly academic qualifications, late of Number 7, The Close, Vicarage Road, Bromley, and now believed to be living in or near Teignmouth in Devon where his Bromley solicitors had last corresponded with him when they had acted for him in the sale of his Bromley house.

Nothing disreputable was known about the doctor, a confirmed bachelor, a heterosexual academic and recluse. During his term of service with the Special Operations Executive Staff throughout the 1939–45 war he had become engaged to another member of that organization, but since the death, in Buchenwald Concentration Camp, of his fiancée he had remained unwed.

All this, Moloney pondered, wonderingly, had been extracted by the amazing Miss Carlsen, in roughly six hours, by some magic of her own plus the amazingly varied number of contacts that the bright young woman had access to.

After a satisfyingly romantic midnight call to Elaine in Paris, Moloney slept the sleep of the much jet-travelled and caught the Cornish Riviera Express from Paddington the following morning. Lunch on the train proved to be better than average, so it was with a comfortable feeling of satiety and good-will towards all British Railway men, that Moloney stepped down on to the stone-lined platform at Teignmouth Station and took a taxi to the 'Burleigh House, Private Hotel'.

A double-fronted, late Victorian merchant prince's sea-
side retreat, this small and well-run hotel was known only
to a few selective people, who often spent whole winters
down in Teignmouth, which was normally far warmer
than London. Here, then, was where Dr Macmillan had
retreated while the sale of his Leonardo sketches was being
completed – and here Moloney hoped to find him.

The landlady was a Mrs Montagu – the widow of a
retired judge, who had turned her hand to providing
excellent food and comfortable shelter to appreciative
guests whom she only accepted on the strongest recommendations. It was not snobbishness that prompted these precautions, for money and position alone could not guarantee a
place on the waiting list for vacancies. What counted the
most was rather whether Mrs Montagu happened to like
you as an individual. She accepted recommendations to
take in other guests only from people whom she already
knew and liked.

That she liked Moloney became quite obvious in the
course of her conversation and she gave the journalist a
detailed account of the three months that Dr Macmillan
had spent as a guest at Burleigh House. It was evident to
Moloney that the lady had been quite attached to her
academic guest, as she happily prattled on about his quiet
ways and charmingly old-fashioned behaviour, speaking of
him as a valued friend. In fact Moloney got the impression
that, had Dr Macmillan been so inclined, the relationship between his landlady and himself might have become far closer.

The most interesting piece of information which the
forthcoming Mrs Montagu provided was that Dr Macmillan had decided to stay permanently in Teignmouth
and to that end had bought a house – exactly where, she
didn't know – but she did remember the house agents who
had sold it to him because she herself had recommended
them.

Moloney only escaped with difficulty from the further

reminiscences of the still attractive widow, but was in time to catch the house agents just before they closed and, by dint of considerable blarney, to extract Dr Macmillan's new address.

Playing a hunch, Moloney decided that valour was the better part of discretion and the taxi once more deposited him outside a front door – this time the imposing front entrance of a beautiful Nash-designed eighteenth-century vicarage on the very outskirts of the town. A plump, cheerful housekeeper answered the door and, on hearing that Moloney had urgent business with the doctor, and having satisfied herself with the journalist's impressive credentials, she showed the Irishman into a large, log-fire warmed drawing-room-cum-conservatory and bustled away to fetch her employer.

Moloney looked round the splendid high-ceilinged room, with its glorious view of a fine garden, terraced in long flights of lawns eventually to hang poised above a wooded valley below. The soul of the Irishman warmed with joy, as he studied the simple but marvellously conceived landscaping of that beautiful garden, shaded by just the right number of carefully cultivated trees – many of them rare and of foreign origin – all blending into God's gift of an English garden.

'Beautiful, isn't it?' said a clear, deep voice behind him and Moloney swung round, unconsciously smiling, to face Dr Macmillan, who had quietly entered the room.

'It's magnificent, sir,' said Moloney, automatically giving the distinguished, frail figure of the scholar the respect which his gentle presence invited.

'Landscaped by Capability Brown no less, and, if I may say so, a small masterpiece in its way. I constantly wonder at my undeserved good fortune in finding such a setting for my final home on this earth. I assure you, Mr Moloney, they will only remove me from this delightful spot feet first.'

'I quite see your point, Doctor,' Moloney remarked. 'But,
by your reference to a home on this earth, you almost
imply that you come from another planet!'

The doctor chuckled – a comfortable, reassuring sound
which clinched Moloney's now growing conviction that,
no matter what the outcome of his enquiries might be, this
slender, prematurely-elderly academic was possessed of total
integrity.

'Forgive me for intruding on your time, sir,' he apologized, 'but I've come about the Leonardo sketches.'

'I thought for a moment you were about to say "about
the smell on the landing" – as I believe the music hall
expression goes.'

Moloney laughed and somehow both men immediately
knew that they could place complete confidence in one
another.

'Mr Moloney, may I invite you to stay the night? The
hour is getting late and I have much to tell you. No! No! I
will hear no excuses. Mrs Winthrop, my housekeeper, is an
excellent cook. I have some fine Burgundy which I think
you might enjoy sampling and lastly – may I say – I find
these long winter evenings somewhat lonely. I really would
appreciate your company.'

Had Moloney wished to refuse, he could not have
resisted this sincere invitation from such a charming man –
and Moloney was anything but unwilling to accept joy-
fully. He paid off the taxi driver, and handed his overnight
valise to the amiable Mrs Winthrop, and by the time he
had made his way upstairs, the Irishman found that the
efficient housekeeper had laid out his pyjamas and dressing-
gown, while his slippers warmed by a cheerful fire which
was now crackling away in the west-facing guest room.

Having bathed and shaved, Moloney dressed again,
marvelling at the old fashioned and splendid hospitality of
his intriguing scholarly host, and went down for dinner.

Dr Edward Macmillan might just as easily have been

born in the Age of Reason, or the early nineteenth century or – and here Moloney found himself almost believing it – at the time of the great Leonardo, for the strange gentle inquiring face had about it a timelessness which is only found in men who have discovered some of the innermost secrets of nature.

After dinner the two men, now completely at ease, retired to the drawing-room, where the log fire provided a glowing background to their coffee and brandy. At last the scholar spoke on the subject closest to Moloney's excited heart.

'I'm afraid that what I am going to tell you will be hard for you to believe. May I first assure you that it is the truth, as far as I can recall it, and I am sure it will not be outside the experience of quite a number of people alive on this planet today.

'I am a qualified physician and psychologist – having qualified at St Bartholemew's Hospital in the late 'thirties at rather an advanced age for a medical student, I'm afraid. I would have gone on to read for my degree in Psychology, had not the war put paid to my decision in 1939 to study at the University of Bonn.

'During the war I was not called upon to practise military medicine but, as my late mother was Alsatian by birth, and I happened to be fluent in both German and French, I was enrolled in the ranks of the Special Operations Executive; mainly through the good offices of my friend, Colonel Maurice Buckmaster.

'Of the operations I was engaged in I shall say little, as I'm sure that it would bore you, but in 1943, while working in occupied France, I was severely wounded, and my life was saved by a Russian émigré named Sergei Lubovitch – known to our group as "Gaston" and one of the bravest and finest men I have met in my life.

'While he nursed me back to health, hidden away in a cellar near Blois, Sergei and I talked of many things and found mutual delight in the extraordinary similarity of our life paths. We had both been pupils of Gurdjieff, the Russian mystic – how I hate that word but it must suffice. We had been born on the same date – oddly enough, at the same hour – exactly ten years apart, Sergei being the elder.

'Among other things we were both fascinated students of Abra-Melin magical rituals, though Sergei was also a practicant whereas I was merely a scholar! You may recall the strange magical society "The Golden Dawn" founded at the end of the last century by Dr Wynn Westcott and eventually almost destroyed by Alisteir Crowley, who quarrelled violently with one of the original founders, Liddell Mathers. Their struggle – both materially and astrally – put paid to an esoteric society of considerable promise, whose members included many famous names, including Sir Gerald Kelly, the painter, and W. B. Yeats and latterly my Russian friend.

'Sergei had attempted and successfully carried out a series of astral projections by which he was able to lift his conscious mind-entity out of his body, and move about in space and time, returning at will – to recall exactly the diverse experiences that he had witnessed.

'You must accept, Mr Moloney, that the deliberate projection of the human psyche out of the body is quite different from a dream experience, though there are, perforce, some apparent similarities. For one thing the astral experience is totally logical and for another it is controllable by will. It is also mortally dangerous and should never be undertaken without long and careful preparation, and then only by someone who has complete control over his mind – and a very strong will-power – along with a high sense of morality. In other words, it is not an area of activity to be entered by the merely curious. An asylum is too often the final home of the appalling mindless results of such unprepared attempts at astral travelling. Suffice it to say that Sergei taught me well and I was able to leave my body at will.

'These activities, and our long enforced proximity, happily resulted in a lasting friendship of the very best kind. We could see each other's faults, forgave them completely, and appreciated each other's good points.

'After the war, I at last fulfilled my ambition and enrolled at the University of Bonn as soon as it re-opened its doors to international students, of whom I was the most mature – in age if not experience. Four years later I received my Doctorate of Philosophy, for my paper on "The Results of Experimental Telekinesis and Extrasensory Perception, Outside the Accepted Mathematical Laws of Chance". Had not Carl Jung personally read and approved my work I doubt very much if I would have been granted my Doctorâte!

'My mother had died after a long illness, and I had inherited sufficient means from my father – a specialist in the physics of optics – whose patents still bring me in a useful income. Thus I was self-indulgently free to continue my researches, provided that I did not marry and start a family – for which I was becoming a little too mature – too set in my selfish bachelor ways! I only found one woman in my whole life with whom I could joyously have shared my destiny but she died . . .

'It was in 1954 that, through the long friendship which I had enjoyed with that remarkable scholar and adventurer, Dr Henry Pulitzer, I found myself concentrating on an experiment of which that interesting Austro-Hungarian fully approved – a close study of Leonardo da Vinci – from first-hand observation!

'Don't look so startled, Mr Moloney! I told you there were things that I had to say which you would find difficult to believe.

'As a Celt you will be familiar with the mythology of your ancestors, and must be aware of the illusory nature of what men call the "real" world. That is, if I read your character rightly?'

'Yes, Dr Macmillan,' said Moloney in a low voice. 'I have followed you quite easily so far – you haven't made any statement which I could not believe. I have some awareness of out-of-the-body experiences, after I participated in an astral projection, during a major operation in my youth. I fully accept what you say!'

'Good, Mr Moloney! Then I can now tell you that, some ten years ago, I finally succeeded in controlling my astral journeys both backwards and forwards in time – as well as in space.

'I believe that as we are part of the total event which comprises our space/time continuum so, to a greater or lesser degree according to our state of awareness, we can observe any part of that event, whether it be in the present, the past, or the future. This is what the oriental philosophy calls "The Akashic Record". '

'I agree,' nodded the Irishman. 'As a "creative" writer, for want of a better description, I frequently find myself "seeing" events which have as yet not taken place and then – some time after I have written about them – sure enough, they happen, just as I described them.'

'Exactly! And the same applies to the past. All that is necessary is the ability to control the projection of the astral, from the start of the out-of-the-body experience, till it safely returns – without psychic damage – to the body which is its temporary home.'

'I would accept that absolutely,' agreed Moloney. 'And I do see the dangers!'

'Splendid! Now, as to the method that I used to bring about the projections. This consisted of total concentration upon a series of tattvas, or coloured shapes – such as the square, the triangle, the crescent and so on superimposed on a square card of a highly contrasting colour. This colour/shape combination produces an effect on the retina of the eye which "The Golden Dawn" initiates referred to as "Flashing Colours", and the result is a rapid disorientation of the senses – or, if you prefer it, a quickly induced trance state.

'With this really quite simple system, and by the use of a "focus" – that is to say some artifact or visual image of the period that I wished to observe – such as an Egyptian Ushabi figure, or a piece of archaic Chinese jade – I found that I could pinpoint the era that I wanted to view with remarkable ease and accuracy. I put this down to the psychometric values of each particular object which, from its manufacture to the time that I held it in my hand, would have recorded events of which it had been a part – rather like a four dimensional recording machine.

'Confident of my rationality and my ability to handle these techniques, I now proceeded carefully to pinpoint my astral projection into the Florence of Lorenzo the Magnificent – in other words I started my experiments in out-of-the-body visitations to the time of Leonardo da Vinci! Do you still follow me?'

'I do indeed!' breathed the fascinated Irishman. 'Presumably, as you could not use an object from the future to act as your mind focus, you attempted a pinpoint navigation of the past. But why the time of Leonardo, Doctor?'

The scholar smiled. 'I had always held his work in the highest regard – after all Leonardo da Vinci was the greatest genius of his age – and there are many sides to his incredible abilities that we have little knowledge of, owing to the loss of his invaluable records which were left in the safe keeping of his great friend Vincenzo Melzi who, sadly, passed them on to his feckless son. I put the tragic dispersal of the great master's work in the same category as the loss to the world of the great libraries of Alexandria and Istanbul when they were burned down.

'Franz Pulitzer was, of course, an authority on Leonardo's work and my friendship with him also decided my course of research.'

'How did you go about it? Obviously your visits to

Florence played a part in your researches.'

'Precisely! I had long before decided that the best and most obvious environment for a projection definitely limited to a given area of the past, would be best obtained by undertaking the experience *in situ*. To that end I went to Florence and, acting on Dr Pulitzer's instructions, confined my research to a part of the city where a ruined monastery reputedly held close associations with Leonardo. Pulitzer believed that the master painter had used part of the building as a studio and, as he himself was a sensitive, my friend had visited the ruins and "picked up" – if I may use that description – a definite feeling that the story was true and that, indeed, Leonardo had at one time worked there.

'You will have to accept these rather sweeping statements at their face value. I assure you, Moloney, that I found them to be true.

'As you know I made my base at the Pensione Armadeo, where I found an undisturbed "safe house", as I would have called it during the last war. The Armadeo family were hospitable, honest and considerate and believed me to be an eccentric English scholar whose hobby was amateur archaeology, which I suppose wasn't too far from the truth.

'The whole setting of that ancient part of Florence was highly conducive to successful astral projection of remarkable accuracy as far as time and location were concerned, and my experimental sessions, which I had linked with the summer solstice, were highly rewarding.

'Even on my first visit I was able to conduct out-of-the-body experiments with pinpoint accuracy and, indeed, I found myself able to view the passing parade of the Florence of some four hundred and fifty years ago.

'The importance of the solsticial effect I shall leave unexplained as it requires quite intricate calculations to demonstrate, but, as you will no doubt be aware, the solstices and equinoxes have always been highly significant throughout man's history.'

'How long did it take you before you actually saw Leonardo?' Moloney could not refrain from interrupting.

'That was on my second visit – an evening that I shall always remember. Two nights previously, as I seemingly hovered over the streets of that city long past, I thought I had caught a glimpse of him as he walked purposefully down a colonnaded street, but the emotional shock of excitement brought me back to my body. Then, during the third consecutive night's projection, I managed to control my emotion rigidly and, sure enough, I found myself clearly observing the great man as he walked, deep in thought along the same street.

'Of course, we only have sketches of Leonardo da Vinci – some by his own hand – but his presence was unmistakable – not least because of the obvious deference shown to him by the people around him.'

'Could he see you, or were you in some way invisible?' asked Moloney excitedly, for he knew that he was dealing with a man whose sanity was not in question and who was telling the truth, as he knew it.

'Normally, of course, a projection is as invisible as a radio transmission but, by will, the projector can make his presence known; this I did, inside Leonardo's studio at the precise moment of the summer solstice.'

'Dear God! What happened?' blurted out Moloney.

Macmillan chuckled at the memory of that moment. 'He crossed himself – and cried out some sort of banishing evocation in monkish Latin! Forgive my amusement – I am in no way belittling the enormous impact of that moment – but to my astonishment the great master thought I was a demon or some other diabolical manifestation – a bitter blow to my pride, I assure you!'

'What in God's name did you do?'

'I did precisely that! I invoked God's name! I crossed myself and attempted to convey to the startled Leonardo that I was no denizen of the Pit. It seemed to reassure him and for some time we gazed at each other in mutual wonder. I shall never forget the image that he made standing in the centre of the floor of his studio, wearing the long gown of the scholar, some fur at the collar being the only indication of his wealth and position.

'His face exactly resembled the sketches which he left to posterity. A fine high forehead; lowering bushy eyebrows framing the brilliance of the large, almost unblinking eyes that seemed to see everything; a noble beard and the great mane of silver hair and, above all, those beautiful hands, strong and capable and immensely sensitive. I shall never forget that moment!'

'How did you communicate? – Could you speak his Renaissance Italian – or did you use Latin?'

'In astral projection there is a certain similarity to dreaming, at least in the method of communication – the channel is, of course, pure thought and the degree of transference relies on the ability of each entity to convey meaning by imagery and symbolism. Strangely enough it seems so natural to us as we dream during sleep, that we never question, at that time, how we communicate with each other! In the case of a mind like Leonardo's, communication was only limited by my own ability to project and focus my thoughts. As far as he was concerned, *his* thoughts flooded in upon me in eager waves, for he soon recognized that I was a projection of the future.

'Communication was broken off, for the rest of that visit, by the very force of these mental exchanges across the centuries. In my excited eagerness I had forgotten the strictest discipline of astral projection – that is never to allow the energy loss, consequent upon the tremendous mental concentration, to go beyond the limits determined by age and health.

'I became ill and nearly suffered a stroke, while the exhaustion induced a physical state which had little resistance to any germ or virus, and I caught pneumonia which very nearly killed me. The Armadeo family refused to allow me to be taken to the hospital, but nursed me with the aid of their family doctor. They pulled me through the crisis and flatly refused to let me go back to England, till I was fit again. They are truly wonderful people!

'The next year I returned, in good health, and with a vital lesson learned. I was determined, somehow, to obtain concrete proof of my mental exchanges with the great man.

'I arrived three days before the solstice, hoping and praying that, in *his* time, Leonardo da Vinci was still in Florence. The astral projection, twelve earth hours later, went without a hitch and once again I found myself back in the Florence of the Renaissance and in the presence of Leonardo. I explained, as simply as I could, that my time, limited by health, was all too short, and the object of my visit was to bring back to the twentieth century some proof of our contact.

'Leonardo saw the value of such an experiment – for posterity to him was like the family that he never had. On his studio table were some of the rough sketches on which he had been working, based on the ideas and concepts of the future which I had shown him by mental transference. I asked the great master for two of the drawings, which I had been impressing on his mind and which contained the last concepts of the twentieth century that I had managed to delineate in my imagination and of which he had immediately grasped the essential principles.

'The plan was simple. Leonardo would place these two drawings inside two separate lead pipes and seal them safely from deterioration. He would then bury them in the small cellar-like cave which lay beneath his work-room-cum-studio on the ground floor of the monastery.

'All this I successfully suggested to him, during three consecutive nights of transcommunication. Then, sadly I hope for both of us, we bade each other farewell for the last time, and I returned, exhausted but safe, to my body in the bedroom at the Pensione Armadeo.

'It was the last time that I could make the journey – but I knew that my task was completed and that now it was up to the Fates to decide whether the experiment was to be a success.

'I slept for a whole twenty-four hours, till I felt completely rested, and then set out for the ruined monastery. The first day that I searched among the ruins, I failed to find anything resembling the cellar/cave of Leonardo's time – but then another brainwave came to me, and I remembered what Franz Pulitzer had once shown me. This was a method of "dowsing" – which is really searching, using bent metal rods, made out of – of all things, wire coathangers – cut and shaped like a capital L, with the right-angled short arms held between the fingers and resting against the palms of either hand. The operator, who requires some practice, then tunes in to whatever he wants to find by visualizing it and, by carefully covering the entire search area, he will find the rods react by crossing each other when he is above the target of his search. That, oversimplified, is the rough principle of that form of "dowsing" and one that I had managed to acquire under Franz's tuition. The result was quite amazing and, that night back in my sitting-room, I opened the cylinders which I had located in the rock-blocked portion of the ruins that had once been the cellar beneath Leonardo's studio workshop. Apart from the most minor of chemical changes in the ink and some slight discolouration of the paper, the sketches were perfect!

'I discreetly hid my triumphant feelings and returned to England, by way of Paris, where I had already determined that I would take the sketches to Sergei who, since Franz Pulitzer was desperately ill, was the only other person that I could trust completely and who would understand how I had found them.

'It was he who persuaded me to sell the sketches in order, as he wisely put it, to give the world notice of their discovery. Had some unscrupulous collector got his hands on them, the same fate might well have befallen them as had happened to so much of the great master's work and they might have disappeared into a private collection and never been seen by the public at large. I saw the wisdom of his advice and, knowing his financial position to be unsound, persuaded him to accept the substantial commission which I knew they would earn him.

'The rest you know. Tragically, Sergei became fatally ill with all the excitement, and had to hand the details of the auction over to Madame Verlaine. The sketches fetched a surprisingly large sum and Sergei's sister is now able to live in comfort on the commission due to her brother. I myself have made quite enough to last me for the rest of my earthly life and I have been able, as you see, to provide myself with this very lovely house and everything I need for my studies and simple research. The remaining funds I have left as a bursary for young students at a university where I have worked, and I consider this to be the true inheritance left to posterity by that wonderful Renaissance man – Leonardo da Vinci.

'Well! There are the bare bones of the matter. What have you to say?'

'Doctor,' said Moloney, almost reverently, 'I believe every word you've told me. I shall never be able to put it down as a newspaper story, but it would make a marvellous short story, a work of fiction. I'll certainly write about some of it, giving due credit and emphasis to your *research* work and, of course, I will submit the article for your approval before letting my editor see it.

'However, there is one small point that slightly worries me – if that is the word to describe my reaction. These drawings of Leonardo's – the submarine, the helicopter, the diving suit, the shells, machine guns and all the other extraordinary objects that he drew – none of them exactly delineates the actual invention as it exists today and as you must have described it to him. Why is that?'

The elderly scholar laughed – the full, rich laugh of a well-balanced mind seeing the folly of vanity in clear perspective.

'That's my fault, Mr Moloney! You will remember I told you that, in astral projection, mind communication can only be achieved symbolically – by the power of thought – and this, of course, is limited to each individual's ability to create accurate images in his mind. I lack that gift to a sad degree. You see, my friend – I can't even draw a straight line!'

Quality

'WHAT MADE YOU CHOOSE this particular magazine, Sir Henry, when you had the opportunity to take over the control of practically any other similar publication?'

The earnest young reporter's National Health glasses almost shone with sincerity, as he leaned forward eagerly to catch and record the Press Lord's reply to his breathlessly respectful question. He could hardly believe his good fortune in having been given this opportunity to meet the great man in person, and to be permitted to interview the billionaire on the subject of his latest Fleet Street acquisition.

The very important person who, up till that moment, had remained apparently unmoved by the young reporter's questions, grunted hollowly and shifted his considerable bulk on to the edge of the massive leather director's chair in which he sat, behind the even more impressive marble-topped desk.

'Aah!' he rumbled, 'I can answer that question with one word: quality! It's the quality of the magazine that counts.'

'Quality,' breathed the stoop-shouldered young reporter,

as he scribbled the key word into his brand new spiral-
bound note book.

'Yes – the quality,' continued the billionaire pensively.
'That is the single deciding factor that I found in that
particular publication – and, believe me, young man, in the
final analysis it is – and I say it yet again – the quality that
counts! That will be all, Perkins!'

The portly newspaper magnate waved a dismissive hand,
indicating the end of the interview with a curt nod of his
large, silver-maned head. The interviewer stammered his
thanks and slid his undernourished, acned self out between
the double doors of the Managing Director's suite.

As the heavy doors closed behind him the billionaire
reached down and, from a middle drawer of the great desk,
took out a silver-framed photograph. Placing it in front of
him, the great man leaned back into the creaking comfort
of his vast leather chair and silently surveyed the picture for
a full minute. Then his massive shoulders started to shake
and his chest to heave, until his whole body quivered in
the grip of some deep compulsive emotion.

At last, as though dragging itself from a great depth, his
voice burst out with a rumbling chuckle that quickly broke
into a torrent of roaring laughter. As he looked through
tear-filled eyes at the photograph of a pretty young woman
– obviously pregnant – smiling out of the Art Nouveau
frame in front of him, his guffaws slowly subsided into a
deep chuckle.

'All those years ago!' he mused, his thoughts wandering
happily in a pasture of memories. 'We'd only been married
a couple of years!'

His wide, generous mouth – a rare feature in a successful
business tycoon – grinned broadly at the reminiscences.

'Let's see! Jean would have been about twenty-three
years old then, and six months pregnant with Marianne at
the time! We were going down into the country to see
Jean's old ballet teacher.'

His thoughts rambled among the details, as one rum-
mages among the litter of a neglected attic.

That was right! The train fare to Tunbridge Wells had
taken their last few shillings, leaving them with only
enough for the gas and electric light meters in their tiny
bed-sitter near Victoria Street. A struggling young writer
in those days, he had just about shot his literary bolt, without finding a financially rewarding mark. He and his pretty
young wife Jean were subsisting mainly on her earnings as
a ballet dancer, along with the revenue from the few
magazine articles that he had so far been able to sell.

Then the baby had started and Jean, now six months
pregnant and prettily reminiscent of a ship in full sail, was
causing him the anguish of knowing that he was not
managing to provide her with the right kind of food to
ensure her health – and that of the baby. Their small stock
of savings had almost gone and they had been faced with
the prospect of a winter weekend with precious little to eat
in the flat and with just about enough money left over for
the weekend's lighting, heating and cooking.

It was Jean who had solved their temporary problem by
suggesting that they should take up her old ballet mistress's
long-standing invitation and visit her in Tunbridge Wells.
They hurriedly re-counted their pennies and found that
the project was just feasible, provided that they walked to
Waterloo Station. A short phone call to Madame Marashkova at the school clinched the matter, and within a couple
of hours they were in the train, clicking its way over the
rails on a cheap weekend return run to the famous Kentish
spa town.

At the station, Madame's daughter, Anna, had come to
meet them in the battered station wagon that did service
as the ballet school bus, and soon they were enfolded in
the warm and slightly hysterical bosom of Madame's marvellous White Russian family entourage, which ranged
from the elderly matriarch of a grandmother, who flatly

refused to speak English, right down to the toddling charms of Anna's little daughter Illona.

Russians, White or Red, are very outgoing and open about physical matters, and delight in passing highly personal remarks about pregnancies, hysterectomies, miscarriages and other intimate bodily conditions. The Marashkova family was no exception, and the Saturday and Sunday of that happy weekend passed in animated conversation about babies, false pregnancies and associated subjects, while Henry was delighted to see his young wife enjoying the generous Slavic fare, provided seemingly endlessly from the Marashkova kitchen.

Sunday evening came round all too quickly for the two young Londoners and, as Henry had to go to an important interview on the Monday morning, the Marashkova family had to say their farewells in time for the last train which was nearly missed, owing to the Russian habit of tearful, protracted goodbyes (Russians never expect to see you alive again). It was only by the skin of their teeth, assisted by Anna's almost maniacal fast driving, that they managed to clamber aboard the last train of the night as it pulled out of the station.

As Henry and Jean flopped down, heavily laden with a huge shopping-bag of food and wine and reading matter thoughtfully provided by the kindly Marashkova family, both of them suddenly realized that they were faced with a dire predicament. Jean, in all the rush and panic of their last-minute dash, had not had time to spend a penny, either at the school or on their arrival at the station, and, now they were sitting in a non-corridor railway carriage in a non-stop train.

As they sat in the empty carriage while the train gathered speed into the rain-lashed darkness of the winter night, they realized the awful truth. The journey would take at least thirty-five minutes and Jean would never manage to last the distance.

As the grim fact dawned on them, Jean and Henry reacted in natural accord with their individual characters. Jean burst into tears while the resourceful Henry burst into frenzied activity.

By now the rain was pelting down heavily on to the carriage roof and splashing wetly against the closed windows – adding yet another, psychologically stimulating urge to Jean's growing desire to relieve her well-filled bladder.

Henry's fruitful imagination had already formulated and rejected the idea of Jean thrusting her backside out of the open carriage window and watering the already soaking Kentish countryside, while he steadied her with his arms as she balanced herself on the window sill with a shapely leg on the seats either side.

He discussed the idea briefly and graphically with Jean, causing her tears to turn into watery giggles and nearly making her lose what little control of her tummy muscles that she still had left. His next thought was that the shopping bag itself might provide the answer, at least temporarily, but this proved to be a somewhat elderly affair made of plaited straw.

However, as Henry turned out the contents hurriedly on to the carriage seat and gazed meditatively at the packages of pirochkis, fruit buns and cakes, and the full bottle of red wine that lay in front of him, his eyes lit on the tightly rolled packet of magazines that lay among the food and drink, and he grinned happily.

'Mrs Murray! Old Mrs Murray at the sweetshop in Folkestone – God bless her!'

'What are we going to do?' wailed Jean desperately, knowing she couldn't hold on to her water much longer.

'Don't worry, darling!' cried her husband, busily tearing open the rolled papers. 'Paper cups, darling! I'll make paper cups! Like old Mrs Murray used to put sweets in at the little corner shop.'

'Will it work, darling? Oh! Hurry! Please hurry!'

Jean's frantic pleas drove Henry on to prodigious feats of dexterity as, like some demented Japanese origami expert in the throes of creation, he folded the outer covers of the stouter magazines into cone-shaped paper cups with rolled up ends.

He had completed nine of these paper confections before his wife's urgent cries made him realize that he must test them out immediately, and he quickly handed Jean two of the cups, which she held close underneath her as she squatted down on the floor of the compartment.

Giggling hysterically, Jean filled cup after cup with a seemingly unceasing flow, which Henry only just kept ahead of with his supply of paper cups. As each container was filled as safely full as it could be, Henry, with one eye fixed on his fountaining wife, passed the filled cups neatly up to and over the sill of the open window with one skilful flick of his spare hand.

The whole business had devolved into a neck-and-neck race between the number of paper funnels that Henry could make and the apparently unending supply of fluid that still flowed liberally from his pregnant wife. He was irresistibly reminded of an elephant he had once seen relieving itself at the zoo; there was about his beloved Jean the same air of amazing watery abundance.

Eventually the stream died to a trickle – not one moment too soon to avoid an embarrassing disaster, which had already almost been brought about by the pulpy failure of one of the cups, made from an inferior paper. This emergency had been brilliantly fielded by Henry, who promptly popped another – somewhat stouter – cup underneath the offending container.

As the last filled cup was neatly flipped away into the passing rainstorm outside, the two young people collapsed back on to the carriage seats, overcome with hysterical laughter, which continued on the short bus ride back to their bed-sitter. They lay helplessly on their foldaway bed, still roaring with laughter till they fell asleep in each other's exhausted arms.

The next morning Henry, still chuckling to himself and with all nervous tension gone, sailed through a highly successful interview at the office of one of the newspapers that he subsequently owned. From then on it seemed as though their troubles were over. As the billionaire gazed fondly at the smiling picture of his much-loved wife, he reminded himself that, four grown-up children later, he still found her as attractive as ever.

'Yes,' he rumbled contentedly. 'There's no doubt about it. It's the quality that counts!'

Vendetta

Don Carlos Jesus Maria Ortega was typical of the successful Spanish businessman of the post-World War Two era. Tall, overweight, fashionably bearded, with the dark, luminous eyes of the Balearic islander, Don Carlos represented all that seemed desirable in life to the Mallorcan workers, who made up his efficient, well-trained staff. Forty-two years old and already prematurely middle-aged, owing to the combination of lack of exercise and the mandatory over-indulgence in food and drink which is the lot of the successful hotelier, Don Carlos reigned supreme over his pride and joy: the Reina Elizabeth Hotel.

This attractive, glistening white machine for the holiday processing of ever-increasing numbers of winter-chilled sun-seekers, lay just outside the rapidly over-developing building area of Palma. Its success stemmed from the reasonable terms offered by its management, and the excellent service of the staff, under the stern direction of Don Carlos himself.

In one thing, however, this sturdy Mallorcan-born is-

lander was not typical, either of the Balearic Islands or of
mainland Spain. Don Carlos was not married, but lived
alone in discreet luxury in a private suite at the top of his
fine hotel. Every month, he would go by ship to the mainland for a conference with his board of directors – and, it was
whispered (none dared speak it aloud), for a visit to the charms
of some Andalusian beauty. An eminently eligible bachelor,
amazingly it looked as though he never would get married.

Certainly the 'Patron' was not 'invertido'. Even with his
few kilos overweight, 'El Jefe', as he was known, was still
a strikingly handsome man, and there were plenty of young,
slim, good-looking waiters on the staff who might soon
have found themselves the object of the Patron's advances,
had Don Carlos been homosexual.

No! It was certain that the handsome hotelier was *macho*,
and it was a mystery that such a splendid matrimonial
catch should, so far, have escaped the marriage net. Outside the hallowed precincts of the Reina Elizabeth, the
staff discussed the whole puzzling matter, and many were
the varied theories advanced as to why El Jefe had not
entered the child-blessed ranks of the respectably wed.

These conjectures ranged from the newly acquired in-
dependence from the dictates of Mother Church that many
wealthy Spaniards now enjoyed, to the possibility that
something vital belonging to Don Carlos might have been
shot off during his service in the Civil War.

All of these theories were, in fact, a long way from the
truth. Don Carlos Jesus Maria Ortega was still unmarried
because he was inwardly consumed by the burning hatred
of a personal vendetta.

Vendettas are, historically speaking, the province of another island race, the Corsicans, who pursue these family
hate-campaigns with a fanatical fervour handed down from
father to son, generation by generation. They are not unknown in the Balearic Islands, however, though in Don
Carlos' case, it was so well concealed that none of his staff

or small coterie of friends ever dreamt that under the wealthy hotelier's urbane and imposing exterior beat a heart bitter with hatred.

This dark shadow had lain over his soul for nearly twenty-five years, and had been the motivating force in his flinty determination to win for himself a prominent place in the island's rapidly expanding holiday industry.

His story starts with the appalling poverty of his birth in a small hovel, in a picturesque but comfortless little fishing village, in the isolated north of the island. His mother died of child-bed fever shortly after he was born, and his fisherman father, drinking copiously in his grief – when he could afford to – soon afterwards was drowned in a savage coastal storm. Little Carlos was brought up by the lean, hard, but kindly fisherfolk of the tiny port and, as soon as he was old enough, went out with the fishermen to earn his living.

Mallorca, in the 'twenties, had only just started to receive and cater for a small influx of foreign visitors. This advance guard of the legions to follow soon became winter residents in the handful of elegant villas which they built, but not even the most far-sighted could ever have guessed at the vast holiday catering industry that one day would bring wealth and chaotic development to the wild beauty of the Balearic Islands.

By the mid-'thirties, however, Mallorca had started to become the winter venue for a number of well-off European sun-seekers who were finding the Côte d'Azur of the South of France too expensive. After the Spanish Civil War, the island's holiday traffic began to expand in earnest and Carlos, who had become one of the war's severely wounded casualties, soon found himself a part of the new catering business.

He was, by then, twenty-four years old and had become a trainee waiter at the Reina Isabella hotel, which graced a small sheltered bay just to the west of Palma. This charming building was set in extensive and beautiful gardens, which

fell, in a series of colourful terraces down to the small
rocky cove and sandy swimming beach below.

The hotel itself was not old and originally had been
constructed as a grand villa for a wealthy, eccentric Spanish
mainlander, just before the turn of the century. Only after
his death, in an aeroplane of his own design and not very
skilled construction, had the villa been turned into a hotel
by the new proprietor, a retired hotelier from Madrid.
Along with the hotel the new owner had also acquired the
fine antique furnishings, and the whole place made a
splendid winter retreat for the visiting foreign guests.

Carlos Ortega's transition from half starved fisherman
to trainee waiter had been brought about by the war. Like
all young Spaniards, he had been called up for military
service in his late teens, and had quite happily embraced the
hard but reasonably-fed life of a conscript soldier in exchange
for the unrelenting struggle against the sea and starvation
that made up his tenuous existence in the fishing village.

With that extraordinary ineptitude that seems to be part
of military administration the world over, this young expert
sailor was not drafted into the navy, but found himself
enlisted in the army, as a trainee-cook. The young fisherman
had adapted himself philosophically to this unexpected line
of quasi-military service, and, as he was blessed with a
quick mind and a naturally hard-working constitution, he
soon learned the basics of army catering and found himself,
within weeks, working as a waiter in the officers' mess of
the island garrison. He also learned to read and write
properly, having previously had only the most simple
education, given to him by the nearest local priest in a
twice-weekly session which entailed a long walk of some
five kilometres each way.

On the outbreak of the Civil War, Mallorca had become
almost immediately the scene of General Franco's initial
landings. He had brought over with him a small force of
fanatical Falangist troops from that other group of islands,

Las Canarias, and soon he had taken over the Balearic Islands as well.

Carlos found himself part of an invading force destined for the Spanish mainland, now that Mallorca had fallen to the General after only a token resistance. In those days the young fisherman had found life too demanding in terms of plain survival to take much interest in politics, and his only teacher, the Jesuit priest, had never inculcated into his pupil any beliefs or dogmas except those which were acceptable to the Church.

Thus an almost totally politically naïve Carlos went off to fight – to be thrown into the savagery of that most horrible of all human conflicts, civil war. With his quick reactions and fine eyesight, he soon became one of the élite front-line riflemen in the bloody struggle for the control of Spain.

In 1936 he had his first experience of killing in hand-to-hand combat when he bayoneted a young Republican soldier of about his own age. The dying soldier's hand convulsively closed on the trigger of his rifle, and Carlos was seriously wounded in the groin. As he lay in pulsing waves of semi-conscious pain in the shell hole, blasted shallowly out of the rocky Andalusian battlefield, he was unable to wrench his horrified gaze from the bloody mess of his tragically young opponent's face. One of his bullets had smashed the Republican soldier's eyes from his head before the rifle had jammed and Carlos had resorted in panic to the use of the bayonet.

Hour after hour Carlos lay, too helpless to move, praying for relief from the sight of the appalling human carnage that he had wrought which lay like a smashed tailor's dummy before him. At last he was found by an American ambulance team operating under the International Red Cross, and taken back in a shrapnel-scarred converted hearse to a field dressing station, where, somehow, an overworked military surgeon saved his life and manhood.

For months afterwards Carlos was in a hospital on the mainland, till the war was over and, at last, he could walk without the aid of sticks. Three weeks later the young ex-fisherman limped off the ferry to Mallorca and back to the struggle of civilian life.

His experience as a waiter in the officers' mess and his knowledge of basic cooking on a large scale earned him a place as a trainee waiter at the Reina Isabella hotel which, now that the Civil War was over, had reverted from the convalescent home for wounded soldiers that had been its wartime function.

Don Ricardo José Ramirez, whose military service had been confined to running an excellent mess for the General Headquarters staff, quickly recognized that the young man was both intelligent and willing to work hard, and he put him in charge of the dining-room's junior staff.

The 'Don' in the head waiter's name was, of course, a courtesy title that everyone rigidly adhered to, and the pernickety but efficient little tyrant ruled the dining-room with a rod of iron, relying on fluent tongue-lashing, rather than his far from imposing size, to enforce a rigid discipline. This was naturally reinforced by the fear, which all the staff had, of losing their jobs and joining the ranks of the island's starving unemployed.

Soon the young Mallorcan was only limping when he became exhausted, and, by diligent hard work, had become the official second-in-command to the dreaded Don Ricardo. Now he found himself handling part of the banqueting arrangements, as well as helping to run the main dining-room. These functions were the occasions of weddings, confirmation parties, birthdays and other anniversaries of the many military functionaries and their families whose financial future had become assured with the victory of the Generalissimo.

So Carlos drifted along in the island sun, working hard enough and long enough to retain his position, but not

whole-heartedly devoting his energies to rising any higher
in the catering trade than the summit of his modest ambition
– which was to become, one day, the head waiter of the
Reina Isabella, and then settle down and probably marry
one of the pretty maids who worked at the hotel.

So far he had not fallen in love, though such a handsome
young potential *novio* would have admirably suited any
of the lovely island girls that he had met. Carlos flirted
with them, by force of circumstances rather than by any
fierce urge to consummate his manhood, whereas they
almost flung themselves at the tall, rugged-faced ex-fisherman – but, truth to tell, his severe wound continued to pain
Carlos for some time after the war, and his tough upbringing
together with the horrors of the mainland war had left the
young man emotionally exhausted and, as yet, with the
deep reservoir of his love and passion untouched.

That is to say, until the Marchmont family arrived at the
Reina Isabella. They had booked into the hotel for the
whole of the month of June.

Captain Marchmont was a typical product of an English
public school, followed by Sandhurst Military Academy,
where he had obtained his commission in King George the
Fifth's service. He made a tall, angular figure, whose strong
face and sinewy hands bespoke the man of action, while
the military precision of his striding walk and his habit of
firmly holding his hands at his sides, proclaimed him for
what he was – a professional career soldier.

Mrs Marchmont was slim and purposeful, with attractive,
clear blue eyes and a practical, neat page-boy hairstyle,
while her gentle voice and natural charm marked her out
from the ordinary run of horsy military wives.

Her daughter was the best possible combination of all
that was attractive in these two good-looking people, but
whereas in the mother there were charmingly well-balanced
features, in the daughter there were all the ingredients of
real beauty. Sixteen years old and in the full fragrance of

her youth, Elizabeth Marchmont walked into the dining-room of the Reina Isabella, and straight into Carlos Ortega's heart. From the moment that he seated the Marchmont family at table number seven by the window overlooking the garden, he could scarcely take his eyes off the girl.

His training, coupled with the natural dignity that so many of the true islanders have inherited from their Moorish and Jewish ancestors, helped him to conceal his strangely excited emotions. No one except Carlos' closest friend, the young wine steward, Miguel Quintal, could have guessed at the racing emotions that passed through the waiter's mind and set his heart in fiery turmoil.

After dinner – the first meal the English family had taken, since their arrival on the ferry from Barcelona – Carlos sat on the bed in his attic room, and tried to make sense of his jumbled emotions. Again and again he asked himself the same question: why should he at the age of twenty-nine, in the fullness of his manhood, surrounded by mature and desirable young Spanish women, find his long-dormant passions aroused, so suddenly, by the sight of an English schoolgirl?

But then again, what a schoolgirl! Her dark brown, pageboy-cut hair framed her perfectly sculptured features, and her eyes were quite startling in their blue clarity. Elizabeth had an infinitely gentle face – the face of a young Madonna, with none of the chubby virginity of the religious paintings in the Mallorcan churches, but warm and sweet and infinitely desirable, as she hesitated on the threshold of womanhood.

The hot summer month seemed to race by for Carlos, as day by day it became clearer to him that he was deeply in love – just as it became clear to Elizabeth's mother that her daughter had become infatuated with the handsome young Spanish waiter.

Mrs Marchmont did not confide her concern at this turn of events to her husband, because the whole idea seemed so absurd, but she felt an increasing sense of alarm that this apparently simple case of infatuation might not be as harmless as it seemed, and that only the family's approaching return to England would solve the problem.

Captain Marchmont had no idea whatsoever that anything was amiss with his family, and continued to enjoy his leave among the beauties of the craggy coastline landscape of the as yet untouched island.

As the summer days sped by, Carlos and Elizabeth, without a word passing between them beyond the normal civil greeting, fell ever more deeply in love, until their longing for each other shone like fire in their eyes – the deep, tiger's-eye brown ones of the young Mallorcan and the sapphire blue of the beautiful English girl.

Miguel spoke seriously to Carlos. 'My friend, you can't go on like this! You hardly eat and you drink nothing. Por Dios! Carlitos, you can't be serious – you, who can have any girl in Palma – and yet you fall in love with a girl whom you can never marry! Think, Carlos! Where is your good Mallorcan hard-headed common sense? Madre de Dios! You are heading for big trouble. Que problema!'

Miguel's open face furrowed with a worried frown as he tried to express his concern for his friend and room-mate, but he only succeeded in making Carlos withdraw further into his own thoughts – thoughts which were now obsessed by images of the lovely Elizabeth.

He found his restless, intermittent sleep filled with fantasies of passionate love-making, with the girl's slim beauty responding to his every longing desire. His waking day-dreams became haunted by glimpses of her lovely, gentle face, so that he scarcely knew whether he was seeing her image or herself.

Don Ricardo noticed his normally smoothly efficient assistant's sudden bouts of clumsiness, and put it down to *la grippe*, the sudden ferocious Mallorcan 'flu which seizes the body and shakes it like a terrier with a stick.

Carlos snatched every opportunity just to catch a glimpse of his adored Elizabeth, as she played tennis, or swam or rode one of the nearby hacienda's horses which were hired out as hacks for the hotel guests. She could hardly fail to notice the discreet presence of her avidly watching admirer – and, being the normal girl that she was, Elizabeth could not resist playing to her gallery of one – while her mother anxiously watched and worried, but being wise, did not interfere.

It was eventually *la grippe* which decided the next move in the game and brought things to a dramatic head by laying Mrs Marchmont low and confining her to bed. The Captain called in the hotel doctor, who made sympathetic sounds and prescribed aspirin, kaolin-morphine, and rest.

With her mother in bed and her father preoccupied with the solicitous care of a good husband, Elizabeth suddenly found herself unexpectedly free from constant family surveillance. In the normal course of events the girl would not have strayed far from the path of deeply inculcated virtue, but the combination of hot sunshine and the passionate glances of her strikingly handsome admirer swept her off her neatly-brogued feet. She and Carlos met in the deepest shade of the remotest part of the garden, and, within moments, were kissing breathlessly.

All the young Mallorcan's bubbling fountain of love came welling up in those passionate embraces, and both of them were caught up in the whirling spiral of natural desire that breaks through all the bonds of caution.

There her father found them and the game was played out in sudden violence and bitter tears. The Englishman, blind to anything but the immediate necessity for self-administered justice, beat the young Mallorcan unconscious, then dragged his horrified, helplessly-weeping daughter back to their suite. The rest of the day passed as a nightmare for both the young lovers, with the Marchmonts

railing against their hysterical child, and the father demanding the instant dismissal of the stunned Carlos.

The next morning, the Captain and his lady, accompanied
by their sadly dejected, still weeping daughter, left the
Reina Isabella to catch the first ferry to Barcelona, while an
embittered Carlos limped out of the hotel, his whole life
changed. The young islander's emotions raced madly within
him – a violent, swirling mixture of love and hate – and it
was with this terrible inner conflict barely under control
that a grim-faced Carlos Jesus Maria Ortega made his
solitary way to the mainland.

He never heard from Elizabeth again and his pains-
takingly slowly-written letters, in laboured schoolboy
English, were returned, unopened, to the Barcelona hotel
where he had found work. The shock of finding and
immediately losing his true love, coupled with the ignomin-
ious beating, had wrought a complete change in his eager
young soul. His love turned sour within him, to ferment
into the bitter brew of a hate-filled ambition. By God, he
would show them all! By Jesus Christ he would make them
realize that he, Carlos Ortega, was a force to be reckoned
with!

Carlos now wanted success and power as passionately as
he had once wanted Elizabeth, and, this time, he pursued
his goal with an unswerving determination. The business
climate of Barcelona was perfectly suited to such a single-
minded purpose, and soon Carlos was well on his way to
becoming the banqueting manager of one of the largest
hotels in that busily ambitious city.

With his growing success he took full physical satisfaction
from the women who crossed his path – starting with the
prettiest of the hotel chamber maids, and progressing along
a swathe cut through the willing hearts of some of the most
beautiful women in Barcelona.

By 1948, Carlos Ortega had become the managing
director of the great hotel, and returned to Mallorca with

a large fortune and his still hotly burning ambition. He
promptly negotiated for the old Reina Isabella and, having
successfully purchased it at a good price, he set about re-
building it into a magnificent new hotel which incorporated
the charm of the older building as an integral part of the
new venture.

In 1952 the new Reina Elizabeth, as he named the hotel,
had opened, with instantaneous success. Travel agents
clamoured for block bookings for their eager clients, for
the British holiday market was investing heavily in package
deals. Naturally, the British believed that the name Reina
Elizabeth had been chosen in honour of their new sovereign,
and no one guessed the real reason for Don Carlos Ortega's
choice.

Despite the passing of the years, despite the achievement
of the ambition he had sworn to fulfil, the hatred and
bitterness still festered inside him. Even now his vendetta
had not exorcized itself. True! The British travel agents
almost grovelled in front of this cool, self-assured, Mallorcan hotelier, as they strove to book their package tours into
his fine hotel. True! The Reina Elizabeth was always full
and invariably over-booked, with a long and eager waiting
list. There was no doubt that the predominantly British
hotel guests enjoyed their visits to the full. Certainly they
greeted their host with respect and admiration.

'Good morning, Don Carlos! We're having a marvellous time, Don Carlos! We'd love to come again next
year, Don Carlos! What a wonderful hotel, Don Carlos!'

All this should have been soothing music to his tor-
mented pride – but, somehow, in his soul, the Mallorcan
still searched restlessly for the fullness of his revenge – and
in the spring of 1954, the opportunity came.

One morning, as Don Carlos idly scanned the names of
the guests arriving on one of the cheaper package tours,
his eyes caught and held two names – those of Colonel and
Mrs Marchmont. His heart leapt as he read the 'package'

details – twenty double and single rooms at the lowest rate
that he would take for the hotel – calculated to the last hundred pesetas, and only available at the very start of the season, when the weather was uncertain. At that time of the
year, the hotel, which Don Carlos habitually closed for redecoration, had just reopened, and, as yet would not have
worked itself up into its fully efficient stride, so he allowed
a few cheaper package tours in until the real season got
underway.

If this was indeed *the* Marchmont family – at least the
two parents on whom he thirsted to revenge himself – then
how different their fortunes must be now – how changed
their situation! He would personally choose their room –
the one with the most restricted view and the noisiest
plumbing – here his mind fantasised some of the other
subtle indignities that he would inflict on the objects of his
hatred. At last, the hand of God seemed to have delivered
them into his power!

Certain that the Marchmonts would never recognize the
former assistant head waiter in the distinguished, bearded
director of the Reina Elizabeth, Don Carlos Ortega could
hardly contain himself as the climax of his longing for
revenge all too slowly approached.

Jesus! How he hated them! They had robbed him of his
one true love – his Elizabeth! – whose memory the charms
of a hundred passionate and beautiful women had never
managed to erase. My God! How he would show the
Marchmonts!

Don Carlos left strict instructions with his manager,
Señor Antonio Garcia, that all arrangements for Colonel
and Mrs Marchmont were to be the subject of his own
personal direction. Then he waited, consumed by a gnawing
impatience as the date for the fulfilment of his vendetta –
March 7th – drew nearer.

When the day finally came his unusually brusque manner
scarcely concealed the fires of bitterness that blazed within

him. At last the hour hand circled the fine antique clock in the stately, marble-lined entrance lobby, and the minutes ticked away, until it was time for the hotel courtesy bus to arrive from Palma Airport.

Half-hidden in the lovely, Moorish indoor garden which dominated the hall, Don Carlos watched the bus sweep up to the marble steps in front of the Reina Elizabeth. As it stopped and the bus door opened, with a pneumatic sigh, a small team of porters, led by an imposing commissionaire, quickly moved forward to deal with the incoming luggage, while the driver swung out of his seat to assist the passengers to alight.

Don Carlos narrowed his eyes to focus acutely on each arriving guest, as the driver helped them down – were the Marchmonts waiting till the last? He felt the discreet presence of his manager beside him, but ignored him. *Where were the Marchmonts?* Ah! There was a final movement in the shadowy interior of the bus, and at last someone else was emerging!

It was Mrs Marchmont – there was no mistaking her still-slim and easy grace, so like – a pang of painful memory went through the Mallorcan, like a bayonet – so like Elizabeth! Sweet Jesus! Elizabeth! His eyes suddenly stung with the heat of his unshed tears. But why was Mrs Marchmont the first to alight? Now here at last was the bitterly hated object of his vendetta! Colonel Marchmont was coming out of the shaded bus, into the bright Mallorcan sunlight.

Don Carlos trembled and fought furiously with himself, to stop crying out aloud. Then, suddenly, a rasping sigh escaped him. He stood stock still, an icy calm mounting up his spine, sweeping all his hate-filled images before it.

Mrs Marchmont was helping her husband down from the bus. As she handed the Colonel his stick, he paused, uncertainly, while she pressed the cane gently but firmly into his hand. The Englishman nodded and then, head held high, with his other hand resting lightly on his wife's arm, he began to walk forward, slowly and deliberately, his white stick feeling the way.

Don Carlos closed his eyes against the dreadful image which suddenly blurred his vision: the image of the blinded, shattered face of that other enemy, the long-dead Republican soldier. He breathed out a long sigh and, with it, all the bitterness drained out of him.

'Don Carlos?' inquired the respectful voice of Señor Garcia. 'What room shall I give to Colonel and Mrs Marchmont?'

The Mallorcan straightened his shoulders and passed a handkerchief across his damp face.

'Colonel and Mrs Marchmont?' he said slowly. 'They are very special. Naturally, you will give them – the Royal Suite!'

The Last Charge

THE 'Y' FORM had come through at first light and was being urgently discussed by the Wing Commander Operations, the Station Commander, the Navigation officer of the bomber Wing and the Engineering and Armament officers of the squadron involved.

An hour previously the Intelligence officers had 'clucked' over the 'Y' form, like remote-controlled hens, for this was a Group operation and they were all puppets in the long chain of command from the Air Marshal downwards.

This was *it*, as far as the Squadron was concerned – an operation that they had been specially chosen for, trained for and now, finally, they were to embark on. It was essentially a 'one-off', as the Engineering officer had called it. A single, decisive attack against a specific target of great strategic importance – a chemical plant, in the heart of the Third Reich.

Since its existence had come to light only four months before, a seemingly endless series of bombing attacks had been made upon it. Mass area-saturation night-bombing

had scarcely touched it and now the enemy had grouped
around the area a number of skilfully-constructed decoy
sites, so cleverly designed that they were indistinguishable
from the actual plant itself – even with the new secret H2S
vertical target radar, with which the latest Lancaster Mark
III four-engined bombers had been equipped.

The Americans had tried twice, with daylight saturation
bombing at both high and medium altitudes, and their
heavy losses hardly justified the pitifully inadequate results.

This vitally important chemical complex was concerned
with the manufacture of highly secret substances which
would form the basis for a new and expectedly deadly
'vengeance' weapon. The heavily-reinforced concrete of the
bunkers, with their well-dispersed siting, made them virtually bombproof, and the whole area was surrounded by
heavy anti-aircraft flak guns, which ensured a hot reception
for the high flying B17 Fortresses and B24 Liberators of the
Eighth Army Airforce and decimated the medium level
Boston and Marauder bombers. Casualties had been so
heavy that only top level pressure from the High Command
had forced a continuation of the aerial assault.

R.A.F. Bomber Command had now decided on an all-
out effort to reach and destroy the heart of the plant at
Augesheim with a low-level attack by one squadron of
Lancasters. These were to be stripped down to their lightest
possible weight and to carry only sufficient fuel for a high
speed dash, at tree-top height, by the shortest practical
route to the target and back. This attack plan, which was
unique in its concept, was totally outside the normal scope
of a Bomber Command Lancaster wing and, from the
station establishment, only one Squadron of eighteen aircraft had been finally chosen.

The 'Y' form covered everything from target plans,
bomb loads and fuel to any other relevant operational
information – such as the latest enemy flak reports and
possible night fighter activity.

For security reasons the form normally arrived early in the morning for a raid planned for the same night, but in this case it had come through on the station teleprinter, well ahead of the post-midnight take-off time. The content held few surprises, except for the heart-stopping fact that the target was even deeper into the heart of Germany than had been expected.

This alteration in the attack plan had been made after the discovery that the much-bombed plant at Augesheim was only the pilot plant for the new industrial process; the actual production complex had been constructed, in even greater secrecy, right in the centre of the industrial hub of the Third Reich.

Wing Commander Peter Donovan, D.S.O., D.F.C. bent his still surprisingly youthful, freckled face, frowning over the attack details, while his Navigation officer, Squadron Leader 'Slim' Newhart, D.F.C. – a tall, leathery New Zealander of great commercial flying experience, who had obviously lied about his age – busied himself with the plotting of the routes in and out of the new target area. The trick of this fancy navigation, which only came with experience and careful judgment was to avoid the main concentrations of flak on the route and it sometimes necessitated flying to an unbelievable accuracy and, in this case, low flying at that.

This particular Squadron had been picked because its aircrews were all experienced first-tour men, and most of its pilots and navigators had embarked on their second tour of operations. When one considers that the chances of surviving the first tour of thirty operations was calculated to be under twenty percent, the reason for this individual choice becomes clear. These were not only highly skilled, battle-hardened aircrews, but they were also *lucky* – and this operation, with all its careful planning, needed that indefinable extra morale booster, Lady Luck.

Whether fortune really does favour the bold, or whether

efficient well-disciplined flying and high morale makes its own good luck, is an academic point – these crews all had that very special qualification.

The code name chosen was Brushfire, but unofficially the operation became known to the participating crews as The Last Charge.

Peter Donovan was a tough, stockily-built twenty-seven-year-old, who had joined the Royal Air Force straight from Winchester School, as a short-service aircrew cadet. Trained at Cranwell just before the outbreak of the Second World War, he had, by 1943, completed his second tour of operations with some fifty trips to his credit. Starting his operational flying on Whitleys, those strange, nose-down slanted bombers, Donovan had converted on to Manchesters, the disastrous twin-engined prototypes for the superb four-engined Lancasters that successfully followed them.

His second tour had been completed on the Mark I Lancaster and he had volunteered for this particular operation in order, so he said, to have the opportunity to fly the new Lancaster Mark III. This bomber, with its American-manufactured, but British-designed, Merlin 38 engines, was to become the bomber of the war. Its revolutionary Bendix Strombach two-stage supercharger gave it a hitherto undreamed-of improvement in performance, and the Merlin engines – already action-proven in the Hurricanes and Spitfires of the Battle of Britain – gained added top performance in their new version. Donovan was completely sold on these aircraft.

His close friends, Squadron Leader 'Timber' Woods, D.F.C., Flight Lieutenant 'Tolly' Maxwell, D.F.C., so called because of his phenomenal capacity for Tollemache's Ale and Flying Officer Coddle, D.F.C., inevitably nick-named 'Molly', all agreed with their commanding officer, but in this particular operation they had one reservation. Although the Lancaster was obviously a superb high-altitude night bomber, as a day bomber it had yet to prove its worth operationally – especially in low-level attacks.

It had a lot going for it – long range, with a stripped-down speed of plus-300 miles an hour; extreme manoeuvrability and sensitive control response – all good points in its favour, but it also had snags, the main one being that a hit in the glycol-water cooling system of the engines resulted in immediate over-heating, and the obvious risk of fire if the engine continued to run.

However, the Lancaster could maintain height easily on three engines and once the bomb load had been dropped it could continue to fly adequately on two engines, even though asymmetrically-trimmed flying would be difficult to maintain at low altitude.

All the crews knew that, with one engine feathered, they might make it back home, without altitude, but the whole question became pretty dicey on two engines alone.

To save weight for this operation there would be no mid-upper turret, nor air gunner to man it. The elimination of this comforting midships turret with its twin .303 Browning machine guns, left only two gun turrets to guard the Lancaster from attack. The total weight saved had added quite a few knots to the aircraft's maximum cruising speed at low level, but psychologically the loss of the guns was keenly felt by the aircrews.

The morning slowly wore on while the W.A.A.F. watch-keepers – girls specially selected for intelligence and well-balanced temperament – methodically pieced together and carefully logged all the details of the operational requirements for the following dawn attack.

Fuel and bomb load details had already been passed on to their respective sections, but final alterations in the fusing of the special delayed-action weapons had been received later and passed over the scrambler phones – strange devices, which distorted the normal patterns of the voice into a sort of Donald Duck garbled sound at one end, and restored them to a hollow normality at the other.

Meanwhile the armourers had checked literally every bullet in the linked machine gun belts, from whose cartridge chutes a steady stream of spent cases would soon rain down on Germany, as the belts automatically disintegrated.

The gun turrets came in for yet another complete check for oil and pressure leaks in their hydraulic systems, while all wire connections and contact points were tested for short-circuits.

The engineers had given each Lancaster's four engines a final thorough grease job and every nut and bolt had been tightened and locked, while the hydraulic flaps and brakes were checked and rechecked, until every human endeavour had been made to ensure the success of the operation.

No one apart from the Station Commander, the Wing Commander Flying and a chosen few in Meteorology and Intelligence operations, knew the identity of the target, or, for that matter, anything else concerned with the attack, except for the dreaded words 'low-level', which could mean anything from five thousand feet down to the 'deck' itself. The crews suspected the latter – a true tree-top low-level attack in bright moonlight. This was because they had practised on dummy targets, for over two months, flying around the Lake District at varying heights and making simulated run-ins on an old ruined castle, approaching at high speed, and making low-level passes which barely scraped over the tops of the surrounding fir trees.

The stripped-down Lancasters could top 300 miles per hour in low-level flight – at least for the final approach and run-in to target – while, for the remainder of the long haul in and out of the attack area, they could maintain 280 miles per hour as their best cruising speed.

The elderly, iron grey Intelligence officer, Squadron leader 'Pop' Waldron, M.C., veteran of the First World War, shrugged his bowed shoulders in sad resignation when the target details finally came through. An old wartime contemporary of such exalted commanders as Air Marshal Sir

Arthur Harris, and Marshal of the Royal Air Force Lord Trenchard, Waldron held a privileged position which he never abused. For this operation he had been called to Command H.Q. and had taken part in all the special preliminary briefings and planning sessions, including the ones devoted to the new bomb – the Lance – which was the brain-child of a highly-qualified boffin, as the scientists were called.

This weapon, which was to be used operationally for the first time on the raid, had been designed specifically for attack at low-level against targets defended heavily against *vertical* assault, but relatively less well protected against an unexpected frontal attack.

The Germans believed that their reinforced concrete casemates and blockhouses were impregnable – and so they were, to high altitude attack.

In principle, the Lance was a rocket-propelled, two thousand pound armour-piercing bomb, released in the ordinary way by being dropped from an aircraft, but equipped with four powder rockets in tubes welded on to the four stabilizing fins of the bomb casing.

In operation the Lance would, after its initial release, fall horizontally for a hundred feet and then, before the weight of the bomb caused it to drop nose-down into a normal trajectory, the rockets would fire automatically and propel the Lance, with terrific force, towards the comparatively lightly protected frontal areas of the chemical plant blockhouses.

Until now the Squadron had only practised with concrete-filled full-scale models of the rocket bomb, without firing the booster units and so far, although the ballistics of the falling bombs had been photographed and carefully analysed, no crew, other than the highly secret development team, knew for certain what the bomb could do when it finally became operational. One disturbing fact emerged dramatically. The aircraft making the drop had to get out of the way a bit smartish, or it would be clobbered by the bouncing effect of a dud bomb, should the rockets fail to ignite.

The various pilots agreed that the best counter-manoeuvre in this eventuality was to wrench the aircraft into an immediate rate six turn to port or starboard, as circumstances allowed, as soon as the Lances were dropped. The height most suitable for dropping the weapon was found to be two hundred feet above the deck – anything lower being suicidal and anything higher exposing the attacking aircrafts' bellies to the copious light flak which was expected to surround the target area.

The tactical plan for flying in and out of Germany was to maintain an altitude of one hundred and fifty feet, with obvious adjustments to conform to the terrain and known obstructions en route. Only on the final run-in to target would the aircraft edge up to the dropping height of two hundred feet.

The actual attack was to be made not later than 0800 hours. The Lancasters would then be vulnerable to fighter attack all the way back to the enemy coast, but an escort of Spitfires would meet them as far into enemy territory as the fighters could reach, and then convoy them back to England.

These and many other problems occupied the minds of those few in the know, and every possible contingency that could be visualized had been thoroughly analysed and, it was hoped, dealt with or allowed for.

The crews themselves sweated out the 'mission', to use the American phrase. They were well aware that, whatever final details of the operation were planned, they had to be along the lines of their previous intensive training and, for some reason that they did not as yet know, this operation was laid on for a very late take-off – at least so they sus-pected. None of them realized that the final attack would be in broad daylight – a fact that, for security reasons, had been kept from them.

The 'A' Flight Adjutant, Flight Lieutenant Bill Bendix, D.F.C., was another ridiculously young-looking twenty-two year old, who, like many other very young aircrew, sported as large a moustache as he could grow. His way of passing the dragging hours, since the news of the laying-on of the 'op', was to walk his black retriever, Nags, round the long perimeter track, while he potted at rabbits with a 12-bore shotgun, borrowed from the armourers' air-gunners training stores. This conventional shotgun was supplied with tracer ammunition, which gave its discharges the effect of miniature firework displays and earned its unofficial users the reputation of scaring the game to death rather than actually hurting them.

Still very much a boy despite his heavy responsibilities, the youthful pilot loved the dog and the raw morning's rough-shooting over the frosty Lincolnshire countryside. As yet he had to feel anything more than a normal healthy yen for the opposite sex, and his good looks and open romantic approach to the W.A.A.F.s on the station, were amply rewarded. The fact that this was considered to be prejudicial to good order and discipline, according to *King's Regulations and Air Council Instructions*, didn't enter into it. The service police, and other administrative personnel on operational stations, were handpicked, and carefully turned a blind eye to such relationships, provided some sort of discretion was used. The whole station felt itself to be part of a special team, about to carry out a highly specialized and dangerous job. Good order and discipline were easily maintained, without constant bullshit for its own sake.

Among the radicals in the squadron Bugsy Matson, a Canadian ex-lumberjack and an experienced bush pilot, welcomed the coming trial of his imperturbable nervous system and rattlesnake-fast reactions. Now a Squadron Leader, with the D.S.O. and D.F.C., commanding 'B' Flight, Bugsy had no qualms about the job to be done. He knew that he was good and that he had a first class crew to back him up. His airgunners practised constantly on the range and were crack shots with the tracer shotguns. They all – especially Bugsy's rear gunner Boy Browning, so called on account of his shining pink choirboy face and his amazing ability with the machine guns of his namesake, ate, slept and lived guns, not only their own multiple .303 Brownings but any and every gun that had been known to exist.

Matson's conscience was quite clear as far as volunteering for this operation was concerned, and his crew had enjoyed their intensive training – the beer was good and the W.A.A.F.s far from unwilling. As to his future, well, the Canadian's tough bush-flying experiences had taught him that living for the morrow was a fool's game.

In complete contrast was Flight Lieutenant Terry Staines, D.F.C., whose unlikely pre-war occupation was that of an up-and-coming dress designer and about as unlike the tough Canadian's background as one could imagine – yet his flying was every bit as good and his coolness in battle quite exceptional. The only real problem about which Terry had doubts was whether or not to ask Flight Sergeant Betty Moresby to marry him, and he spent a lot of his time debating the chances of making the attractive little dark-haired W.A.A.F. a widow before he could finish his second tour of operations, which now had only this one sortie to go.

Terry used the last few hours before the briefing taking a long walk with his adoring Betty, who fortunately was off-watch, and they passed the afternoon blissfully together in the remoter parts of the perimeter of the airfield. Their gentle pilgrimage along the path of young idealistic love was largely an affair of long and passionate kisses, rather than the consummation of their natural longing for each other. They both held back this fulfilment until the day of their marriage, which Betty, at least, had determined would be soon or never.

So the day slipped by – to the aircrews in general all too

slowly, to others in the ground crews much too quickly to allow them to do all the desperately important last minute jobs.

The sweating armourers found that something had gone wrong with the bomb release mechanisms of both J-for-Johnny and B-for-Baker, involving the Armament officer, Flight Lieutenant 'Bombs' McKay, in some loud and descriptive swearing as he urged on his frustrated crews to almost impossible efforts.

A freak accident had also taken M-for-Mother temporarily out of the operation; a sheet of corrugated iron, loosened in the previous night's gale, had suddenly torn loose from the hanger roof and crashed down on to the starboard outer engine of the Lancaster beneath, just as the 'chiefie' was supervising a run-up to full power. No one was injured, but the accident meant a propeller change, as the unbalanced engine had nearly torn itself loose from its mounting before the apoplectic Flight Sergeant could get the panic-stricken leading aircraftsman engine fitter to shut down the power.

One aircraft unserviceable out of a total of eighteen might be acceptable, but by no means could three aircraft be taken off the operation. The armourers' crew heaved and strained at the reluctant bomb releases, until at last the mechanisms responded to the full satisfaction of McKay's perfectionist demands.

This sturdy Glaswegian was among the ablest technicians in the Command, and he well knew the importance of the new weapon, from the detailed briefings which he had attended with the chosen few at the H.Q. Their words now came back to him, with the utmost clarity:

'*Lance is not just another experimental bomb – therefore it cannot be allowed any chance to misbehave. Should there be a hang-up the weapon must be brought back out of enemy territory, before being jettisoned. We cannot afford the chance of one of these weapons falling into German hands.*

'*Remember – the bomb normally will become live in the first fifty feet of its fall after leaving the aircraft. Within the next fifty feet the rockets will ignite with their pressure fuses operated by a barometric device and, at an estimated altitude of one hundred feet above the ground, Lance will follow a flat trajectory with terrific acceleration into the target.*

'*The usual safety device of an air-turned propeller in the nose of the bomb, ensures that it will only become live after leaving the aircraft's bomb-bay and, due to the high dropping speed of the aircraft, the bomb doors will be blown off first by specially designed charges.*

'*The resultant drag from the abnormal airflow will be greatly reduced by the modification to the airframe in fitting a streamlined deflection device forward of the bomb door. This has already been successfully tested and found to give quite adequate results – the speed loss and manoeuvrability effects are quite appreciable but, in this particular operation, are acceptable.*

'*Any malfunction of the rocket mechanism will result in an inadequate impact on the blockhouses and, therefore, the failure of the weapon, which will then become an ordinary Armour Piercing Bomb.*'

McKay's sigh of blasphemous relief finally escaped him at 1600 hours, when both his armament crews reported 'weapons stowed and operational – all aircraft bombed up'.

The night closed in and, at 1900 hours, the briefing finally took place in the Wing Operations Room. This consisted of a well blacked-out, prefabricated, asbestos-walled hut, built as an adjunct to the solid concrete security of the pre-war station's operation block.

The aircrews, consisting of pilots, navigators, bomb aimers, engineers, gunners and Signals wireless operators, totalled a hundred and twenty-six in all. The customary pre-briefing chatter was unusually subdued and, when the Station Commander, Wing Commander Flying, and other top operations staff entered, there was an equally unusual smartness in the way the aircrews came to attention. It was as though they all felt, unanimously, that this operation must be played strictly by the book.

The briefing would, in retrospect, hold a peculiar poignancy for the aircrews under Donovan's command. It was, still unknown to them, the first low-level daylight formation raid that Lancasters were to attempt since the near-annihilation of Squadron Leader Nettleton, V.C.'s desperate raid on Augsburg.

The Wing Commander jumped on to the briefing platform and drew the curtain aside from the huge operational briefing map, which was covered with transparent sheets of talc, marked heavily with red Chinagraph symbols denoting flak areas and enemy fighter airfields. The route itself, so carefully planned to minimize or avoid both of these hazards, was clearly marked in black tape, starkly prominent on the giant coloured patchwork of the large overlapping charts. Its indication of the depth of penetration into Germany provoked an immediate gasp of surprise, which was quickly suppressed as the crews realized its import.

Donovan spoke shortly and to the point, wasting no time on unnecessary formalities.

'This operation is code-named Brushfire and is designed to take out the latest and most dangerous enemy threat to the war effort. This is a large chemical plant, which has been built here, at Magdasburg, a hundred miles further east of the original pilot plant at Augesheim, which, so far, both the Americans and ourselves have failed to eliminate. In the station operations room are all the relevant target details – and the latest Photographic Reconnaissance Unit photographs – taken forty-eight hours ago. Study them thoroughly.

'We will attack in six waves of three aircraft each, as we have been practising. The time over target will be 0800 hours tomorrow morning . . .'

A second, quickly choked reaction broke from his crews' tense throats.

'Make it a good prang – good luck. Engine starting time will be 0330 hours.'

The Wing Commander was followed by the duty Intelligence officer, acting under a special briefing from Pop Waldron, who stayed quietly in the background. F/O Williams was an ex-journalist and could marshall and present his facts briefly and clearly.

'The target is heavily defended with light, medium and heavy flak units – but Command believes that, at nought feet, your run-in to target and the aiming point will be below the normal maximum depression angle of the heavy guns. So too with the medium flak – leaving the main defence to the light guns. Command is therefore one hundred percent certain that only light machine guns and single light .20 millimetre cannon will constitute the main hazard to this totally unexpected low-level attack, once inside the target area. The enemy are not aware of the existence of our new rocket-propelled Lance.

'You will bomb on a heading of 175 degrees magnetic, at the aiming points marked on the target photographs next door. There is also a relief model of the target area which will give you a good picture of the plant and your turning points into – and beyond – the target. Remember! You must turn on to your last course here – clearly marked by the four tall factory chimneys at Ebshaven that will give you an exact fix for your run-up to target.

'Your indicated airspeed to be 300 knots – giving you a four minute run-in to the aiming points. Drop your Lances at 200 feet altitude – no more and no less – then immediately turn away with a rate six to port or starboard, climbing steeply to clear the peaks either side of the valley below.

'A diversionary raid to keep Jerry busy on his night fighter front, will be carried out by 350 Lancs and Halifaxes of Bomber Command. All aircraft will drop the usual "window" radar-confusing metal strips – on the way out of

Germany and this will coincide with your low-level raid on the way in.

'At your altitude, down on the deck, you will be well below enemy radar and the "window" drop will effectively drive Jerry mad. Therefore, your reported sightings will have to be by enemy ground observers only and, at the speed you will be going, this method will be too dodgy for Jerry to plot your next move accurately – hence the "wiggles" en route.

'All escape and evasion gen is available in the Int/Ops office. Make sure that you all have your escape kits. Good luck.'

The Meteorological officer, a scholarly academic who constantly forgot to do up his uniform jacket buttons, gave the squadron an up-to-the-minute weather forecast of thick alto-cumulus cloud over the target area by dawn, which would provide some useful cover for the raid.

'You will have a thousand feet or even lower cloud base, but it's just possible that the plant's own chimney stacks will be pouring out sufficient vapour to lower this cloud base still further. Either way it's not an easy picture for enemy fighter interception.'

Armament and Engineering plus Signals came next in the briefing line – each giving the final details in their particular field. Then, well out of the usual order of things, came the Navigation briefing. The gaunt New Zealander's clipped, nasal tones spelled it all out.

'Every attempt has been made to avoid the main flak areas, but an error of two miles off track will, nine times out of ten, position you within range of an intensely defended factory or any of the many military areas which cover Germany thickly at these points. Only your speed and close, ground-hugging tactics will carry you through. This is very much a navigators' raid: pinpoint navigation is your speciality – tomorrow it will be the main means of your survival. Kia-ora!' The Maori words for 'Good Health' came naturally to this quiet man, in whose hands the lives of a hundred and twenty-six young flyers now rested.

At the close of the last technical briefing the Station Commander, Group Captain Neil Trentham, D.S.O., D.F.C. spoke:

'We are proud to have been chosen for Operation Brushfire because it is so vital to the safety of these islands and to the outcome of this war. New explosives, the like of which we have never known, are being manufactured in this chemical plant. It is your job to make certain they never will be used.

'You have had training for two months for this raid and you have behind you many hours of operational flying. I have personally seen the final tests on Lance. It works – and it's up to you to see that it is delivered on to the target. Use these weapons successfully and you will have made a tremendous contribution to the war effort, and to our ultimate victory. God go with you!'

It was the first time that any of them had heard the Station Commander use those words. Almost too old at forty-eight, Group Captain Trentham had flown with the R.A.F. since his early twenties and still battled doggedly with the Group's Senior Air Staff Officer to allow him to fly on operations at least once a month. His fervent request to be included on Operation Brushfire had been turned down flat – so it was an unusual outburst of his normally carefully concealed emotions that caused this highly skilled and experienced bomber pilot to utter those final words.

The aircrews stumbled back through the blacked-out, tree-dotted dispersal sites of their temporary wartime home. Black-out regulations were total on all operational airfields and only the dimmest of dark blue lamps indicated the way to the most vital areas. Apart from these lights – 'Dim as a Toc H lamp', as they used to say in the '14–'18 war – the only others showing were the perimeter markers, which were switched on solely to guide aircraft in or out, and the flarepath lamps that shone out bravely for take-off and landings. These were also sparingly used because of the constant danger of German night fighter intruders homing in on them, to shoot down returning bombers or, better still from the enemy viewpoint, to catch aircraft taking off with a full bomb load.

Some of the crews dispersed to their huts to write a last letter or even to make out a will, while others huddled together for comfort in their various messes; yet none of them drank any alcohol before the operation.

An hour later all the crews sat down to their operational meal, which consisted of real (as opposed to dried) eggs, bacon and coffee or tea with piles of toast and marmalade and genuine butter. Some ate with compulsive appetites, as though knowing that this was to be their last meal, while others were scarcely able to face eating at all.

The Chaplain, Squadron Leader Paul Whittaker, M.C. – known as Padre or the Sky Pilot to most and Saul to his closest friends – watched them all, waiting until they had finished the last crumb of their meal, in case he was needed. A First World War Artillery Captain, the Chaplain had taken Orders between the Wars, worked as a missionary in bomb-torn Shanghai during the Sino-Japanese conflict and had eventually graduated to the R.A.F. As he sat, waiting patiently, he felt something creep into the periphery of his consciousness – a grim manifestation of the darkest side of war. Once again he experienced the chilling terror of a precognitive insight into the immediate future as face after face of the young men seated at the mess tables took on the leaden-grey line and skeletal bone structure of the dead.

With a shudder and a prayer he immediately thrust aside the presence of the Dark Angel; but in that moment of pure horror he knew the price that would have to be paid by the dawn of the morning to come.

Wing Commander Donovan lay on his bunk, unable to

do more than doze fitfully, while a hundred times or more he went over the details of the plan.

Dickinson and Roberts were to fly on his port and starboard quarter and, should anything happen to his aircraft – P-Peter, then Ken Dickinson would be an able substitute to lead the first attack wave. Behind them would come his second in command, Timber Woods, to take over the role of Master Bomber, if needed and, after leading his 'V' formation (Vic) into the attack, to circle the target area, directing the subsequent four Vics on to the target areas where the Lances could do the most damage.

If all the aircraft made it to the target they would be lucky to escape heavy damage from the guns, however they were sited, despite Command's optimistic line of patter, but Donovan had decided that the volume of fire could be divided and therefore reduced to manageable proportions. The answer was to deliver the attack with as many aircraft as possible succeeding each other in Vics of three, all firing together at the defences at ten-to-fifteen second intervals.

From first to last attack by the eighteen aircraft, the operation must not exceed a time-over-target of four minutes. That meant reaching the turning point at exactly the right moment and, from then on, their success and subsequent survival depended on split-second timing and precision flying.

Again and again Donovan's mind methodically went through the names and aircraft identification letters of each of his Squadron pilots until he had their battle order firmly fixed in his memory:

First Wave

Himself, Master Bomber	P-Peter
Ken Dickinson	O-Orange
Harry Roberts	Y-Yorker

Second Wave

Reserve Master Bomber,	
Timber Woods	C-Charlie

Tony Parradine	B-Baker
Cocky McKenzie	R-Roger

Third Wave

Leo Constantine	A-Apple
F/Sgt Markham	D-Don
F/Sgt Acheson	L-Love

Fourth Wave

2nd Reserve Master Bomber,

Bugsy Matson	J-Johnny
F/Sgt Monahan	U-Uncle
F/Sgt Wyatt	S-Sugar

Fifth Wave

Terry Staines	Q-Queenie
Molly Coddle	F-Freddie
Mike Betteridge	E-Edward

Sixth and Last Wave

Bill Bendix	M-Mother
Con Rigby	K-King
Tolly Maxwell	G-George

Although Donovan knew his messmates, by the odd nature of the rapidly changing war, he only knew his non-commissioned officers casually. Warrant officer Con Rigby, a former stage magician, was an exception, as everyone on the station had heard of his prowess with card manipulation, and the odd coincidence of his aircraft being K-King only increased the validity of his personal legend.

Timber Woods, Molly Coddle, Terry Staines and Tolly Maxwell were Donovan's closest friends, while Bill Bendix and Ken Dickinson, who had only recently joined the Squadron, were well on the way to becoming the same. Only Bugsy Matson, the monosyllabic Canadian bush pilot, remained at a distance, but his crew were totally loyal to him and would have had no other Skipper.

Donovan's thoughts turned to the reason for his own absolute dedication to war – the death of his young fiancée, a W.A.A.F. watchkeeper, back on his first tour of opera-

tions. Sgt. Mary Perrault had died in the shambles of the
watch office when a single intruding Junkers 88 had
bombed the station, at the end of 1941. This one incident
in Donovan's life had turned him from a young idealistic
pilot, who flew for the thrill and pleasure of flight itself,
into the cool, dedicated bomber pilot, whose single-minded
drive was directed at killing as many Germans as possible.
Only the Poles and the Czechs, with their implacable hatred
of the Nazis who had raped their countries, matched the
cold killing machine that Peter Donovan had become.

Strange though it was – and it was the same with the
Poles and Czechs – this total, mind-absorbing hatred only
possessed him during the actual operations. In the mess or
in the local pubs Peter Donovan was apparently a normal
young man, and his spontaneous laughter held no note of
hysteria.

The icy blackness of the freezing night closed over the
station high up on the Lincolnshire Wolds. Only the flying
control section and the vigilant W.A.A.F. watchkeepers,
together with the cat-napping Intelligence officers, kept
the long vigil.

At precisely 0245 hours the batmen stumbled round the
dispersal huts with urns of steaming hot tea, sweet and thick
with evaporated milk. The crews, who had been lying fully-
dressed on their bunks, pulled on their flying boots and
shrugged themselves into the bum-freezer Irvine jackets
which they wore, in addition to heavy long Johns, high
necked sweaters and any other warm clothing that they
could cram on under their battle dress. This stemmed
from their normal habit of dressing for high-altitude non-
pressurized flying but, even on the deck, the cold night had
persuaded them to swathe themselves as usual.

Quickly they assembled at their respective crew rooms,
grabbed their parachutes and dinghy packs and slipped on
their Mae Wests over their fur-lined jackets and under their
parachute harness. The fact that these bulky, trussed up,

muffled figures in their layers of protective clothing and heavy harness could react physically and mentally like trained athletes, seemed a minor miracle that defied belief.

Dressed and battle-equipped, the crews were driven out through the Stygian darkness to the dispersal sites where, on tarmac hard standings, the squat shapes of their Lancasters stood waiting. The cat-eyed W.A.A.F. drivers picked their way, their trucks guided by only the dimmest of masked headlamps, depositing each crew at the quiet bustle surrounding its own Lancaster.

As the crews climbed aboard their aircraft, the ground crews were busy readying fire appliances and emergency booster batteries, while the armourers gave a final check to the specially modified bomb doors.

It was now 0300 hours and the eighteen crews were snuggled down into their respective positions, the pilots strapped into their Sutton harnesses, their oxygen and w/t connections tested and plugged in, the gunners encapsulated in the front and rear turrets, the harnesses criss-crossed over their parachute straps. Navigators and Signals were already poring over their compact working areas, checking and rechecking their charts and codes, while the bomb aimers went forward into the nose and, for the umpteenth time, ran their skilled hands over the new bomb sights.

For this trip the bomb aimers would ride all the way in the very front of the aircraft, lying on the padded aiming positions, while they alerted the pilot to the constantly changing conditions of the approaching landscape, leaving the front gunners free to use their guns against the enemy ground defence.

The pilots and gunners alone wore seat-pack parachutes – navigators, bomb aimers and wireless operators all had clip-on chest packs close to hand, to leave them free to move around the aircraft. Only on the direct command of the pilot would they finally attach their chutes, just prior to entering the target zone, or before abandoning the aircraft on the words 'Bale out' which, despite the regulation 'Abandon aircraft', was still automatically used in the final emergency.

Then and only then would the rear gunners crank their turrets round and go out backwards, or centre their turrets and go back into the aircraft fuselage if they were front or mid-upper gunners. Then, like the rest of the crew, they would bale out through the emergency hatch down below and to the side of the pilot's seat or aft, near the rear turret.

The pilot alone would hang on till the last moment, to keep his heavily damaged and probably blazing aircraft flying straight and level – long enough for his crew to drop free. Then usually too late and too low, he would attempt to follow them, for no system of automatic pilot mechanism had yet been devised to act as a substitute for his devotion and skill.

Engine-starting time ('press-tit time' in the vernacular) was nearly upon them, and the crews, their final preparations and check lists complete, watched the hands on their watches and control panel clocks as they ticked off the remaining minutes. Then, at exactly the same moment, eighteen pairs of hands pulled hard back on the control columns to keep the tails down, eighteen fingers flipped open the red switch covers, and away whined the starter motors as port-inner engines began to burst into life, followed by the healthy roar of the starboard-inners, the port-outers and finally the starboard-outer engines.

Some were slightly behind the others, as the bitter cold of the night had clamped its icy grasp on the carburettors, and one or two engines only fired after a heart-wrenching, aimless swinging of the triple-bladed propellers. But finally all eighteen Lancasters pulsed with the heavy throaty roar of their four Merlin engines, and the young pilots and flight engineers keenly scanned the gauges for a magneto drop that might yet take them out of the operation. Even M-Mother, her brand new propeller almost untried, thundered with life; and the full squadron of Lancasters roared defiance at the grim, black March morning, drowning out the endless sighing of the wind as it whipped across the wolds.

Eighteen oddly attractive ugly ducklings trundled their heavily-laden way along the perimeter taxi tracks, led by P-Peter, piloted by Peter Donovan. Eighteen shuddering black chargers, bearing their burden of a hundred and twenty-six young knights, slowly made their way towards the end of the main runway, down which they would soon thunder, to heave themselves up like the Pegasus of legend, and carry their youthful warriors against the Dark Forces who ruled Germany.

In yet another way the slow juddering approach to the runway was strangely reminiscent of the start of another wild charge, by six hundred young men long ago in the Crimea where, at Balaclava, the Light Brigade had prepared to charge the Russian guns, every man, from Brigadier to cavalryman, fully knowing the impossible odds stacked against them. But whether led by Wing Commander Donovan or Captain Nolan, whether six hundred men raced to their destiny on the sweat-streaming backs of galloping horses or one hundred and twenty-six young men were borne to their fate in the cold Duralumin bellies of the roaring Lancasters, the archetypal image was the same. Light against Darkness – just as it had always been and will always be until man learns true wisdom.

In the dimly-lit cockpit of P-Peter, Donovan waited tensely for the green light to shine out from the Aldis lamp of the controller, standing inside the perspex bubble top of his conning position in the control van at the start of the runway. In front of him the runway lights flicked on and then there at last was the light, blinking out an unexpected 'V' for Victory. Donovan let out a grunted 'Go!' as his hands eased the four throttles forward. With his flight engineer beside him, assisting with flaps and other

vital controls, Donovan steered the roaring Lancaster down
the long runway between the lights, racing faster and faster
beside them, till, at the last moment, with plenty of flying
speed to spare, he eased the shuddering aircraft up into the
icy blackness above.

The anxious eyes of the Station Commander watched
the leading Lancaster whistle up into the night – clearing
the trees at the end of the overshoot by a good hundred feet
– then turned to watch Ken Dickinson's O-Orange swing
down the runway as a gust of veering crosswind caught the
aircraft, and then rise into the scattered low cloud above.

Harry Roberts immediately followed the second Lancaster
and, within seconds, Y-Yorker had climbed over the
bordering trees and raced to catch up and align with the
leader.

Roberts's rear gunner, Tubby Andrews, gazed back and
down at the flickering stub of the aircraft exhausts below
and the dim cockpits of the following squadron, as Lanc
after Lanc succeeded them down the long flarepath of the
airfield beneath, now rapidly receding and disappearing in
the ground haze and scudding thin cloud.

The three Lancasters leading the raid closed up into a
tight 'V' formation, with O-Orange to port, P-Peter at the
point of the Vic, and Y-Yorker to starboard. As the three
black silhouettes of the bombers reached the first turning
point, over Mablethorpe, the navigator, Slim Newhart
passed Donovan the new course of 110 degrees magnetic,
and the three leading aircraft swung round, as though they
were one. Behind them the five following Vics performed
the same precise manoeuvre, until all eighteen Lancasters
roared out over the North Sea on a direct line to cross the
Dutch coast a few miles north of the Hague, between Leiden
and Haarlem.

During this first long leg of their route, a 240-mile dash
across the wind-blown swells of the dark grey sea below
them, all eighteen aircraft slowly lowered their altitude from

400 feet, as they crossed the wet sands and foam-washed Mablethorpe shoreline, till they seemed to slide over the crested wave tops at the bare minimum safety height of one hundred feet.

Flying low over water is very difficult, so this precise altitude was maintained by their bomb aimers calling up corrections to the pilot, while they watched two powerful spots of light, thrown forward and downwards from specially mounted under-wing lamps on to the sea below. One light, the starboard one, was green, and the other a yellowy red – both clear and bright and surprisingly easy to pick out on the rolling surface of the sea beneath them. If green passed red to the left, the aircraft was too high, and if it raced beside red on its own side the aircraft was too low. The idea had been suggested by 617 Squadron's successful attack on the dams of Western Germany – though in that case the attack height was only 60 feet and the water surface was practically mirror smooth.

Originally the spotlight/height device had been suggested to the vivid imagination of a young 617 officer, while he was watching the spotlights shining on a dance routine in a theatre – or so the legend went. At all events, it worked well, provided the sea wasn't too rough and, for this operation, it certainly helped the concentration of the pilots as they jockeyed their hurtling aircraft well below the scope of the enemy radar.

So for nearly an hour, bucking an infuriating headwind, the eighteen Lancasters thrashed their way across the already lightening darkness until, just before 0400 hours, the bomb aimer, Teddy Marchant, called to Donovan over the r/t: 'Enemy coast ahead,' and the Wing Commander eased lightly back on the control column, to bring P-Peter swooping across the undulating sand dunes of Holland.

Their landfall was bang on track, just outside Haarlem, and Donovan led the squadron round on to a new course – 114 degrees magnetic – aiming for the next turning point,

just north of Utrecht. Close below them the lattice of Dutch
canals sped past, the glistening wet polders showing up
lighter against the greeny-black ribbons of the thin connec-
ting lines of waterways that are the life-blood of Holland.
The crews could see the small, neatly dispersed farms in the
glow of the false dawn, and occasionally a windmill's
slowly turning sails flashed past beneath the hurtling
Lancasters, while their threshing propellers and the roar of
their passing whirled flights of panic-stricken geese and
ducks up into the swirling slipstream of their wake.

No lights showed – partly because of the strict blackout
and curfew in force throughout German-occupied Europe,
but also because the thrifty Dutch farmers worked from
first to last light, with the minimum of artificial aids, which
were both costly and hard to come by. But suddenly a light
flashed out from some patriotic Dutchman's house, and
the bomb aimer spelled out the 'V' for Victory morse-code
letters, as they scudded past the winking torch on their
port bow.

All this time, apart from brief intervals of r/t exchanges,
the aircraft and their crews had maintained strict radio
silence, their high-speed crossing of the Dutch coastal sand
dunes being the first indications that the German coast
watchers had of their existence.

The unsuspecting anti-aircraft crews had been rudely
shaken out of their nodding watch and now desperately
tried to swing round their guns to fire after the rapidly
disappearing Lancasters, which passed either side of them
to melt into the pre-dawn ground haze that rose off the
polders. The last two Vics, under Terry Staines' and Bill
Bendix's command, experienced some light flak, but it was
ill-aimed and well wide of the mark.

The rough track of their flight path was already being
feverishly telephoned, in excitedly shouted German, to
defence positions in their probable line of flight, and by the
time the squadron had skimmed between the outlying

farms near Utrecht, some light 20 m/m tracers were coming up to intercept them, though still without much accuracy.

Boy Browning in Bugsy Matson's Y-Yorker's rear turret had the satisfaction of shooting out a searchlight, and grinned as his tracer bullets ricocheted off a troublesome gun emplacement, till a stern order, in clipped Canadian, told him clearly and blasphemously to save his ammunition.

In a narrow, swerving arc, the eighteen Lancasters swept round the northern suburbs of Utrecht and Slim Newhart set the new course to pass south of the airfield near Amersfoort and around the outskirts of the small town of Arnhem, as yet only a name on a chart but, within eighteen months, to be written forever in the annals of airborne warfare.

Sporadic fire still blazed up at the low-flying, grey-black shapes, which were now becoming more visible in the false dawn light.

One Lancaster, E-Edward, with Mike Betteridge at the controls, started a blazing fire in the starboard outer engine. Still radio silence was kept by the small fast-moving armada of aircraft, as their headlong rush carried them towards the rapidly approaching German border.

Only the crew of E-Edward knew of their desperate battle to deal with the rush of flames, of the 'Graviner' system's extinguishers' failure to deal with the cascade of flaming petrol that marked their flight path with a long streamer of orange-red fire, making them a clear target for any guns in their vicinity. Tragically, they failed to beat the flames, and the explosion that consumed them was only witnessed by the sixth wave of Lancasters, coming up close behind, and the few horrified Dutch folk who had wakened to the sound of their engines. At a hundred feet the interval between air and ground was short and, three seconds later, what was left of E-Edward smeared a shower of blazing debris across the wet turnip fields south of Amersfoort.

Bill Bendix sent a short w/t message to 'Brushfire Leader'. It simply said: 'E-Edward gone in.' Molly Coddle swung his aircraft, F-Freddie, even closer to Terry Staines in Q-Queenie, till the two Lancasters seemed to make one silhouette.

The sky was lightening rapidly now, as the seventeen remaining aircraft rushed low over the flatlands south of Zutphen Lochem, and roared at maximum cruising speed straight for the German border where, right in their flight path south of Enschede, a German temporary airfield had been alerted.

The enemy radar, up till then, had been totally baffled by the showers of window metallic strips falling from the returning British diversionary high-altitude raid, giving a confused picture of any movement in the airspace above the border. But now, realizing from the reports flooding in that the approaching raid was at ground-level, the German radar crews attempted to obtain fixes on the elusive Lancasters.

Already, Messerschmitt 109 and Focke-Wolf 190 fighters had been alerted at Enschede, and would have taken off to intercept had not nature forestalled them with a dense mist, which rose to ninety feet above the German border, effectively pinning the fighters to the ground.

With their propellers washing deep paths in the top of the thick mist, the Lancasters flew just above its swirling mass, crossing the German border without actually seeing it, and only managing to pinpoint their positions by the solitary church steeples that thrust up, like markers, through the milky fog beneath.

Donovan's track lay north of Ahaus and there he had to make a slight swing south – taking great care not to swerve too far out round the turning point, or he would have led his squadron over the waiting guns of Munster.

The instrument panel clocks had swung round to 0530 hours as the Dortmund Emms Canal flashed by below, the barge traffic seeming to be frozen on the surface, while heavy tracer concentrations started to hose them from an armed barge escorting the vital canal traffic. The curving yellowy-red tracer shells sought for and found their mark in A-Apple, flown by Leo Constantine, who died instantly in the first well-aimed burst.

The dead pilot had convulsively clutched the control column in his death agony, and hauled it back, causing the stricken Lancaster to rear up and, with the front and rear gunners still returning the barge's fire, the aircraft flipped over on to its back and, streaming flame like a blazing comet, smashed deafeningly into a small wood just east of the canal. Donovan transmitted one short message: 'Brush-fire Leader to Lancers – D-Don Markham take over your Vic.'

This was only the second time that the squadron had broken radio silence and the transmission was far too short either to act as an accurate radio direction finding fix or to give away any clue as to their route or target. The Germans were still forced to rely on their visual observer reports, as the remaining sixteen Lancasters rushed headlong into Germany.

Their ally, the fog, was thinning now and at any moment Donovan expected that the enemy fighters would strike, but he knew that one other factor had been carefully con-sidered during the planning conferences, and might now serve them well. Command had believed that the Germans would send up a maximum night fighter effort against the high altitude diversionary attack, and they had been right. This meant that many of the German planes were being diverted, in the misty conditions, to land at other airfields, and Donovan guessed that, in the confusion, a large scale day fighter counter-attack was unlikely to get going immediately.

Meanwhile, another factor had entered into the balance between success and annihilation. This was a five hundred-strong American daylight raid by B17 Fortresses and B24 Liberators on Schweinfurt, unknown to Bomber Command, as it had been unexpectedly advanced by twenty-four hours to impress a visiting Senator from the States. News of this raid had come through Command too late to transmit to Donovan's squadron, which by then was halfway across the North Sea. Donovan, unaware of this new state of affairs, was more than surprised that, as yet, there had been no German day fighter reaction.

As the large American formations flew, ponderously, twenty-five thousand feet above the Dutch coast, every enemy fighter capable of interception, was scrambled by German Luftwaffe fighter squadrons. Staffel after Staffel of ME 109s and Focke-Wolf 190s, mixed with ME 210s and 410s – and even Junker 88s – climbed frantically to head off and break up the boxes of high-altitude American bombers, escorted by their long-range P 51D fighter planes.

This raid, more than any other factor, saved the Lancasters from annihilation, for, as the leading Vic swept round the next turning point, south of Bielefeld, only one 'scharme' of four ME 109s had been scrambled to intercept them, and two of these had collided in the ground mist on take off. So Donovan's low-level raid was only jumped by two ME 109s, which bored in to the squadron with all guns blazing.

Bill Bendix's M-Mother, Con Rigby's K-King, and Tolly Maxwell's G-George found themselves fighting off two experienced fighter pilots, who must have been calling for reinforcements as they came barrelling in for the attack. But shooting down bombers at normal operating altitudes is one thing, and trying to get below a Lancaster, travelling at around 300 knots, a hundred feet above the undulating deck, is something quite different.

The first ME 109 came in too close and paid the penalty, as the four .303 Brownings in each of the rear turrets smashed into its engine and the cockpit behind. The dead pilot slumped forward and the Messerschmitt cartwheeled into a farmhouse, exploding in a shower of blazing petrol and ammunition, with bricks and mortar flying around like giant shrapnel.

As the squadron raced round Bielefeld, Tolly Maxwell in G-George found himself with a dying rear gunner and his plane badly damaged, his port outer engine glowing red hot and his hydraulic system destroyed, so that the wheels and flaps tried to come down at well over their maximum permissible speed. This had the effect of bringing the Lancaster to a shuddering skid in mid-air and both flaps tore away together, swerving the aircraft into a drunken curve which the pilot, with all his skill, could only just correct.

G-George was already out of formation, with the wild swings of its damaged controls, and was far too low for the crew to bale out. Tolly Maxwell did the only thing possible in the circumstances and somehow, either by superb airmanship or incredible good luck, with the wheels still unlocked and virtually hanging down below the inner engines, managed to slow his aircraft's lunging progress further, and plumped it down, in a cloud of mud and churned up vegetables, into a large field. Shedding bits of Lancaster, he ploughed a flat furrow through the turnips, till he skidded to a smoking stop just short of a solid-looking wall.

The German pilot wasn't so lucky and, as he overshot the slowing Lancaster, he was caught in the cross-fire of M-Mother and K-King, to explode in a ball of yellow flame and black oily smoke.

Q-Queenie's and F-Freddie's rear gunners caught a glimpse of Maxwell's crew in rapidly receding perspective, scrambling out of the wrecked Lancaster, as Donovan led the remaining fifteen aircraft around on to a direct course for the Harz Mountains, beyond which the target lay under thick cloud and industrial smoke haze.

The thundering roar of the sixty bellowing Merlin engines passed low to the north of Hameln, where a heavy road convoy, generously protected by multiple light flak guns, cost the lives of D-Don's F/Sgt Markham and his crew and F/Sgt Acheson and his young team in L-Love.

D-Don went in first, blowing up in mid-air and showering part of the German road column with blazing debris, followed ten seconds later by L-Love, which burst into flames, staggered drunkenly, and then, amazingly, canted crazily over on one wing and somehow turned back to crash on to the rear of the road convoy, with a gigantic explosion as its Lances blew up. Whether the pilot, in his last moments, deliberately crashed his stricken Lancaster on to his enemies will never be known, but F/Sgt Tommy Acheson should be given the benefit of the doubt.

Thirteen Lancasters out of the original eighteen tore along just above the outlying suburbs of Hameln, as Donovan lined them up for the straight run-in to the Brocken – the highest part of that end of the Harz Mountains. At this moment the lowering base of heavy black cumulus nimbus clouds burst into torrential rain, drenching the sloping fields and thick fir forests below.

Donovan had no alternative but to climb rapidly and to attempt to skirt the worst of the storm clouds. Their eyes glued to their leaders, the Vics of Lancasters plunged into the least solid-looking of the cumulus masses and, with navigation lights temporarily switched on, they fought their bucking aircraft through the vicious turbulence.

This was flying at its most difficult, with the constant scanning of the instruments balanced by the need to check on their leaders' formation position, and only top pilots could make it out safely into the clear sky beyond the heavy 'Overcast'.

Donovan's rear gunner saw a brief yellow and red belch of flame behind P-Peter, as Tony Parradine in B-Baker swung too wide to avoid his leader's red port wing-tip light, and smashed his aircraft into a jutting pinnacle of fir-tree-topped granite, before exploding into a blast of high-speed fragments of incandescent Duralumin.

The surviving twelve Lancasters surged out of the swirling black storm at 3,500 feet, as Donovan's rear gunner counted them off on the r/t. The Wing Commander cursed and quickly recalculated the odds on the success of the final target run-in. With one third of the attacking force gone it only left the round dozen, with eight Lances each – a total of ninety-six rocket bombs to hurl into the blockhouses of the chemical plant. But the twelve Lancasters might still be able to divide up the defending guns between them, if they formed up to attack in four waves of three.

Donovan's mind was made up and his quiet voice called over the W/T: 'All remaining aircraft – form up in "Vics" to your nearest leader. The Brocken's dead ahead – turn to 185 degrees magnetic and get down on to the deck in the valley ahead – the Ebshaven chimneys are easy to spot. Turn there, then spread your "Vics" into a straight frontal attack, twenty yards apart in threes. Don't acknowledge. Out!'

The Wing Commander crouched over the control column and skirted the mass of the Brocken in a shallow diving turn, picking up maximum speed for the final ground-hugging approach. Dead ahead, the tall brick smoke-stacks of the kilns loomed out of their own smoke haze.

Shuddering under full boost, the howling Merlin engines pulled their streamlined airframes down to two hundred feet, where the new formation steadied in lines of three aircraft, and hurled themselves down the steep valley in parade ground formation.

Donovan thought: 'By Christ! We'll show the bastards how to do it.' Then he clicked on his transmitter switch and radioed one final message: 'All aircraft Brushfire Squadron – *Charge!*'

The strange, anachronistic order seemed totally appro-priate as the Lancasters rushed towards the rapidly swelling outlines of the concrete blockhouses which made up the complex bulk of the Magdasburg plant.

The bomb aimers made their last adjustments to the modified bombsights, while the front gunners rattled off short bursts of incendiary and tracer bullets into the huge maw of the plant, as it swelled towards them.

'Bomb doors gone!' yelled Teddy Marchant, as P-Peter's specially-built expendable bomb bay covers blasted down and away, in a brief flash of crumpling metal, when he fired the explosive charges.

The Lancaster bucked like a wild stallion, till Donovan's sinewy hands once more brought his now wind-shrieking aircraft under control. The air, spilling into the open bomb bay with a high pitched whistle, despite the streamlined hump built forward of the large gap, considerably reduced the final attack speed of the racing aircraft, but still allowed the Lancaster to approach the aiming point at well over 260 knots.

Donovan's bomb aimer aligned the target in the special sight, as the two tall steel smoke-stacks of the chemical plant appeared, centred in his cross wires.

'Left – left!' He almost spat the words into the R/T mask mike. 'Steady! Bombs away!'

For an instant P-Peter seemed to catch her breath with a great gasp as the eight Lances fell away. Then, before the anxiously watching eyes in the following three aircraft, bright orange streaks of flame suddenly accelerated below and ahead of the racing Lancaster and sped, in almost flat trajectories, towards the great grey blockhouses, which now seemed to fill the valley from side to side.

Donovan flung the howling bulk of P-Peter up and over into a wildly vibrating, almost vertical climbing turn to port, thrashing over the great plant and swinging past the tall smoke-belching chimneys to straighten up and pass behind the target, into the wider valley beyond, just as the first delayed-action fuses exploded in the Lances which had smashed into the lighter frontal concrete of the industrial complex buildings. His rear gunner, Tommy Butson, saw great chunks of crumbling cement rising into the air, as the first deeply-embedded rocket bombs exploded; and one whole blockhouse collapsed when the damaged supporting blast-walls crumbled beneath the weight of the heavily-reinforced concrete roof above.

Donovan circled the periphery of the plant, as two Lancasters emerged from the smoke and blast, but he couldn't identify them in the swirling dust of the explosions, as the second drop of Lances blew up in the centre of the plant.

As the first of the two aircraft below him thundered down into the valley beyond, he saw that it was on fire and, at that moment, it burst into a small sun of intense heat, and the flaming debris smashed into the trees below. The second aircraft staggered up out of the valley, and disappeared into the boiling clouds above.

Donovan emerged on the target's frontal flank, just avoiding the steep side of the narrow valley and, with a tight diving turn, joined the last section of three aircraft, as they dropped their twenty-four Lances. These accelerated in multi-streams of flame, ahead of the aircraft, which climbed away to port and starboard, rocking wildly in the super-heated air.

Once more Donovan plunged P-Peter, with all guns firing, into the inferno of exploding bombs, seething smoke-clouds, and flashes of bursting chemical tanks – climbing steeply up into the low swirling cloud base and surging from side to side in the violent turbulence of the fire storm beneath.

As P-Peter cleared the target area for the last time, the Wing Commander saw the remnants of his command burst out of the tumbling clouds of boiling water-vapour and form up, in as tight a formation as possible, behind him. He felt totally drained of all emotion. Hatred, fear, even triumph – nothing remained to him but the instinct to survive and to bring his remaining aircraft back to base.

Dropping down once again to tree-top-skimming height, he gave his engines as much power as they would take, while Slim Newhart handed him the new course to steer, only a trace of the strain of battle audible in the New Zealander's quiet voice.

Tommy Butson's last view of the colossal pillars of twisting black smoke and ravening flames was his final experience of life, as he died quietly in his shattered turret from the dreadful wounds suffered during Donovan's last wild run on to the target.

Teddy Marchant gazed fixedly out of the plexiglass bomb aimer's window as his life blood soaked into his padded aiming-position in the splintered nose of the Lancaster – while, above him, the front gunner, Jock Mackie sat in his wrecked turret, cut in half by a direct hit.

So P-Peter and what remained of the squadron came home, by some miracle, while the German main fighter effort was still concentrated on mauling the heavy American raid on Schweinfurt. Beside her flew Terry Staines, in Q-Queenie, with a dead navigator and two wounded gunners aboard. On the other side, flew Timber Woods, with his whole crew miraculously unscathed in battle-scarred C-Charlie.

Cocky McKenzie, in a faltering R-Roger, followed close behind until he could safely ditch near the English coast, while Molly Coddle flew F-Freddie, with his navigator, Jimmy Hennigan, awkwardly helping him with the rudder controls which his own severely wounded legs could no longer operate.

Others, like F/Sgt Monahan, in U-Uncle, and F/Sgt Wyatt, in S-Sugar, died with their crews in the wreckage of their aircraft, scattered along the route like obscene litter.

Bugsy Matson's crew must have died when he smashed into one of the chemical plant's tall steel smoke-stacks, as his badly damaged aircraft failed to gain height after successfully releasing his Lances. Only Molly Coddle's rear gunner saw M-Mother crash.

Throughout the nightmare flight back Donovan barely spoke. In a daze of shocked reaction he flew his aircraft almost automatically towards the swarming escort of long-range Spitfires that met them at the German border.

Operation Brushfire was over and the secret of Hitler's atomic bomb lay buried in the smouldering ruins of the Magdasburg chemical plant.

The *Daily Telegraph* carried a postscript to Operation Brushfire in its obituary column, many years later.

'The death of Air Marshal Sir Peter Donovan, K.C.G., V.C., D.S.O., D.F.C. (Retired), at the age of 63, recalls the exploit for which he received the Victoria Cross. The daylight raid on the German chemical plant at Magdasburg, which he successfully led, brought the Nazi bid to make an atomic bomb to a halt. The raid proved to be costly in the loss of aircraft and aircrews; out of a total of 18 Lancaster bombers, only four returned to base.

'Sir Peter leaves a widow and one son, Squadron Leader Alan Donovan, Royal Air Force, Bomber Command.'

The dark haired, bespectacled young Flight Lieutenant put down the newspaper as he finished reading the obituary notice.

'Weird thing, the A.M.'s death!' he said, addressing a pretty blonde W.R.A.F. Flying officer, seated beside him in the Mess at Coltishall.

'In what way?' asked the latter-day W.A.A.F.

'Well, Harry Duncan was on duty at the Hendon Air Museum during the R.A.F. Open Day when the A.M. died, and actually got to him first as he collapsed. By the time the M.O. arrived, it was too late – one moment there was the old boy sitting in the cockpit of the last Lancaster in Britain, apparently quite happy and fit, and then, suddenly, he shouted out something really odd and collapsed!'

'What was it?' queried the young W.R.A.F. officer.

The Flight Lieutenant stood up, unconsciously at attention, before answering. Then he said, quietly:

'He shouted – "Charge!" '

Conservation

I FINISHED THE LAST WAR flat on my back in Eighth General Hospital, near Minden, in Western Germany – not as a wounded hero, recovering from wounds sustained in that final battle against the Third Reich, but as a result of a combination of double pneumonia and sheer exhaustion.

Among the efficient and devoted nursing staff there was one Senior Sister who seemed to take more than a passing professional interest in me, and it was due to her kindness and forethought that I found myself on sick leave in Britain, leisurely making my way by slow train to a rendezvous with my ministering angel's brother at Stockbridge.

This stalwart outdoorsman had been severely wounded by an exploding landmine early on in the war, and had, since then, sturdily refused to let the loss of both his legs stop him from helping the war effort in some useful fashion. Turned down for factory work, because of an additional lung injury, he had finally found himself a niche looking after the country's sadly neglected fresh-water fishing grounds.

Surprisingly enough, quite a significant amount of
Britain's need for protein was supplied by fresh-water
fishing, helped out by experimental fish farming and conservation. The traditional salt-water fishing grounds had
become even more hazardous than usual due to the presence
of mines, submarines and enemy commerce raiders. The
fishermen of England, many of them near to and even
beyond the age for retirement, responded as they had always
done in times of crisis, and a great number of them died
under a hail of strafing bullets from enemy aircraft or light
coastal forces, out on forays from the continental coast.

The popular fallacy that fresh-water fishing had always
been exclusive to the wealthy had been given the lie by the
hoards of everyday folk who regularly fished Britain's
rivers when they could get the time off during the season.
In fact, it had long been Britain's number one pastime, and,
since beach fishing had been ruled out by the sowing of
landmines round the coast, more and more fishermen took
to fresh-water fishing, not just for sport but to help out the
larder as well.

Many of the so-called landed gentry had gone off to war,
leaving their families to run their estates and, since the land
was the prime source of desperately needed food, the water
had to suffer, and many good fishing streams were choked
with weeds for lack of attention by a water bailiff. Some of
the efforts of the Women's Land Army were directed at
helping remaining elderly water bailiffs to cope with the
task of unclogging the choked streams and keeping up
stocks of fresh-water fish, but it was a hard struggle. As
usual, faced with a dire emergency, Britain somehow found
the slender resources to meet the worst of these problems,
and among the cheerfully determined volunteers for this
difficult task was my nursing sister's elder brother.

His disability didn't prevent him from driving a converted
fifteen-hundredweight truck, on which had been mounted
a large metal milk container, lined with a thin inner shell of

stainless steel. With the ventilators on top covered over with fine netting, and the tank filled three-quarters full with clear fresh water, this contraption was ideally suited to moving young fish from the badly clogged breeding grounds and the pike lurking in those underwater jungles, down to more open and safer water, where their normal life cycle could continue. Thus, in the summer of 1945, I found myself staying with the 'tin-legged conservator', as he called himself, learning from him the basic principles of fish conservation.

Like Douglas Bader, whom I had seen during the war using his Desoutter artificial limbs with consummate skill as he hauled himself aboard his aircraft, this indomitable man also manipulated his prosthetic legs with an incredible and determined agility that captured my unbounded admiration. His one ambition was to create the best environment possible for the successful breeding of his fresh-water fish and he devoted all his energies to moving young fish into safer waters. The pools which the conservator fished for this purpose lay about a mile or so from his cottage, higher up the River Kennet, and it was to these locations that my new-found friend and instructor took me early one morning shortly after I had joined him. With us we brought the equipment which he used to catch the small fry.

This consisted of large hand-nets on wooden frames, and a 'Chore Horse' electrical generator – a neat little petrol-driven machine, light and easily transportable, that could turn out a sufficiently strong current to stun the young fish unconscious and make them easy to catch without harming them. This was accomplished by floating out a contact-bearing cork and wood contraption, switching on the generator – and lo and behold, up to the surface floated the stunned fish. Off went the generator and into the river we waded in our rubber thigh-boots, and out we came with our hand-nets filled with unconscious small fish, which we then tipped into the water tank on top of the truck. It was simple and effective and I quickly got the hang of it: by the end of an hour, just before dawn, we had already netted and transferred to the tank quite a considerable number of small fry.

At this point the conservator called a halt and we had some welcome rum-laced coffee and sandwiches for our early breakfast.

As Fate would have it, this particular pool was onethat my instructor had, so far that year, left untouched, and as the generator had been playing up, we had left it running for a bit on its own, to warm up on the frosty morning. The anode-bearing wooden float was still in the water, where we had left it switched off after the last catch of fish, and when we had finished our brief meal, the conservator made his way over to the running generator and flipped over the main switch.

As he rejoined me opposite the float, a cheery 'Good morning!' rang out. Our attention was directed across the river, where a small cottage stood on its own, set back from the tow-path. The voice belonged to an elderly, stout, red-faced man wearing an old dressing-gown and slippers.

By his close-cropped, stubbly white hair and upright bearing I idly placed him in my mind as a retired military man, probably eking out an inadequate pension on a tiny small-holding, raising chickens and ducks here in the middle of nowhere. The battered old Ford utility van which stood outside the cottage, loaded with wire fowl coops, bore out my instant diagnosis.

Neither the conservator nor I could possibly have guessed that the cheerful greeting came from a dedicated all-year-round bather – and, before either of us could shout a warning, he had kicked off his slippers, whipped off his bathrobe to reveal an old-fashioned bathing costume, and plunged straight into the river pool where our busy little generator was belting out a lively current of electricity.

As he hit the water he made the light splash of a skilled

diver and immediately vanished deep below the surface, only to reappear almost instantly from the depths with a great rasp of surprise as the power hit him.

In that speechless moment of horrified realization, it was the conservator who reacted first. With a stumbling, swaying run, he reached the generator and slammed off the switch. We stared aghast at the still figure floating, horribly inert, on its belly, the ruddy face looking blindly down into the dark water. Then, with a simultaneous movement, we both made for the river. With my last remaining remnants of reason I managed to stop the conservator diving in — thigh boots, tin legs and all — and clumsily kicking off my rubber waders, I plunged in, fully clothed, and in a few strokes had reached the unfortunate ex-soldier, who lay in the water like a dead whale.

Back I towed him to the bank and together we dragged the poor old fellow out of the water, the conservator's powerful shoulders making light of the work, and, rolling him over on to his stomach, I began to apply old-fashioned artificial respiration.

He had swallowed a lot of water, most of which we got out of him almost immediately, but it took us a good fifteen minutes of hard work before the object of our strenuous life-saving attempts flickered back to life.

The conservator wrapped him in his greatcoat and chafed his hands as I turned the old boy over on his back and reapplied artificial respiration to his chest. As my friend slapped the unfortunate swimmer's cheeks, the old man's eyes at last opened and focused blearily on our anxious faces bending over him.

I shall always treasure those first words of his, as his spirit finally stepped back over the dark threshold and he rejoined the human race.

'It must have been far colder than I thought,' he said.

Neither of us disillusioned him with the truth.

All the Difference

THE REINA ELIZABETH is one of the loveliest hotels in Spain. Although it has become an important part of the great Spanish holiday machine, it still retains a lot of its original charm. The buildings themselves are now a dazzling white whereas, before the last war, they were of a more restrained hue and reflected the slower pace of life of the pre-Civil War Spaniards.

The style of architecture has become a cliché, endlessly repeated by the Get-Your-Place-in-the-Sun costa villas that have spread like a cement fungus, from Barcelona to La Linea. In the case of the Reina Elizabeth, however, a great amount of care had been taken to ensure that the hotel blended into its Mallorcan background, and today, although surrounded by the utility pre-stressed concrete block houses of the island tourist boom, the Reina still stands out as an authentic example of Spanish architecture.

One of the main reasons for this rugged individuality is the large expanse of gardens that surround the hotel, as a moat surrounds a castle. They form a beautifully laid out pattern of trees and shrubs, landscaped to fit the Reina into the *Feng-Shui* of the terrain, with a properly fitted carpet of flowers and shady greenery. (The art of Feng-Shui – the Spirit of the Landscape, literally: 'Wind and Water' – is a Chinese pseudo-science, developed over thousands of years, to ensure that every building, grave, monument and other man-made construction fitted without disharmony, into the overall natural balance of the landscape.) In the gardens of the Reina, a latter-day Spanish equivalent of Britain's great Capability Brown has achieved a marvellously peaceful serenity among the commercial chaos of the island's hotels.

The conclusion that one draws, after enjoying the study of these lovely gardens, is that their landscaping and care is the responsibility of one person, for there is that indefinable sense of wholeness about them that could only have been brought about by a single visionary soul.

Further enquiries would elicit the information that the contracting horticultural firm which looks after the gardens is under the sole direction of a wealthy Mallorcan, Don Enrique Inca.

This man's unusual name has nothing to do with an early Peruvian ancestry, but derives from the name of a small town in the centre of the island, where Don Enrique was born. 'Don', as is so often the case, is merely a courtesy title and he has never made any pretence to nobility by adding the 'de' of the Spanish aristocracy.

In fact, Don Enrique Inca is the antithesis of the current archetypal successful Spanish businessman. Whereas they are usually somewhat overweight, he is as lean and tough as a briar – and, like a briar, his strong body is twisted in shape, making him resemble nothing quite so much as a Spanish version of Richard the Third. His gaunt, handsome features are now graced with a beard, which softens the lines that early hardship and malnutrition have ineradically etched into his good-looking face, while his

whole demeanour and quiet manner arouse respect rather
than pity.

Don Enrique rules his small horticultural empire with
absolute autonomy, and can often be seen taking an active
part in the landscaping of some important new building
project. His services are much sought after, and he always
has a long waiting-list of eager prospective customers only
too anxious to employ his extraordinary skills, for nowhere
on the island is there another person with such green
thumbs. They say that Don Enrique can conjure flowers
out of the bare rock, revive a lightning-smitten tree, or
even save a goat-ravaged garden.

This unusual man is further remarkable in that he is still
soltero (a bachelor) and lives alone, except for a housekeeper and her chauffeur-handyman husband. His villa is
almost a miniature version of the original hotel, the Reina
Isabella, from which the more modern Reina Elizabeth
expanded into its present form.

His small estate lies some distance from Palma in the
direction of Valldemosa, and is perched high up on a rocky
promontory, overlooking the west coast of the island, and
commanding a breathtaking view that Don Enrique quietly
enjoys as he tends his lovely garden.

Here the housekeeper often brings him his lunch: a
peasant meal of panecillos of bread, goat's cheese, and a
porron of the rough red island wine. This midday meal
alone would mark him as a complete outsider among the
newly rich of the island, who regularly over-line their
stomachs and shorten their lives with large business lunches,
followed by long siestas. Every day, when Don Enrique is
home, this simple ritual is performed: Felicia brings him
his lunch, and after slowly and deliberately enjoying it, he
sits for a short time quietly gazing out over the lovely view.

This unusual Mallorcan is not the sort of man to have
close friends, but Don Carlos Ortega, the retired owner of
the Reina Elizabeth – another bachelor – probably knows

him the best, for both have spent most of their working lives at the original Reina Isabella, and then later at the Reina Elizabeth.

In 1933, Enrique Inca was starving in Palma. Desperate for food, he was caught stealing from the hotel's dustbins; hauled up in front of the manager, Don Esteban Montero, he had stood helplessly waiting for his punishment, too proud to beg for clemency and too exhausted to care. His haunted face and crooked frame somehow touched the bountiful streak in Don Esteban's nature, and the great man listened to his story with some sympathy. The upshot was that Enrique became an assistant gardener in the hotel grounds, a glorified hewer of wood and carrier of water, but at least with a roof over his head – a tiny garden shack behind the potting sheds – and, for once in his young life, enough to eat. For the first time since he became an orphan, Enrique found a place that he could call home, and although he scarcely earned any money, he did manage to scrape together a few pesetas to furnish his tiny shack, however sparsely.

It soon became obvious to the head gardener that here was a naturally gifted young man, whose understanding of plants and trees was quite exceptional. Enrique, however, was not an easy person to get to know, for he was deeply conscious of his twisted frame and had, consequently, withdrawn into himself, to a point where he found it hard to communicate with others.

For the next few years, the young hunch-back devoted his waking hours to laying out and tending the hotel gardens till they took on an individual beauty which was very much of his own creation.

The Civil War left Enrique unenlisted, as his obvious deformity precluded him from being called up for military service, and the dreadful savagery of that appalling conflict might seem to have passed him by without touching. This was not so, however, for Enrique was deeply sensitive, and when the Reina Isabella became a wartime convalescent home for wounded soldiers, the young gardener saw to it that each bedside table was graced with a small bunch of flowers or a single lovely plant.

When that ghastly war of attrition was at last over, and the great nations paused for a moment from their participation in the slaughter, which they were using as a dress rehearsal for the world-wide blood-bath to come, Enrique found himself chief assistant to the old head gardener, who was now on the point of retiring.

The old man, Manuel Salem, a frail, walnut-brown Mallorcan ex-fisherman, had lost his own son, Antonio, in the bitter fighting at the Ebro, and had now, unofficially, adopted Enrique as his heir. That year he retired and, as is so often the case with folk who have worked hard all their lives, passed away after only a few months of unaccustomed leisure.

Enrique felt his loss deeply, for he had come to love the old man, who throughout the years had been kind to him and had willingly passed on the knowledge and experience that had made him such a fine gardener.

The hotel had meanwhile reverted to its original role and, after redecoration, had been reopened to the small influx of wealthy mainland and foreign patronage.

The position of head gardener was now vacant and the logical and wise choice would have been Enrique, but the new manager – an ex-army Colonel who had been given the job as a reward for services rendered to the Falange – couldn't countenance the post of head gardener being filled by someone who had never done military service, and who was a crook-back as well. To sack Enrique would have been too foolish, for his knowledge was invaluable, so the Colonel kept him on but appointed another ex-soldier – a one-time quartermaster sergeant – to be in command of the Isabella's 'horticultural logistics' as he now redefined the job of head gardener.

This proved to be a mistake, for the new non-commissioned commander of the Isabella's gardens was an alcoholic, and spent most of his time – and a considerable part of the funds set aside for horticulture – drinking with various old ex-service cronies, until he became insensible. The hard work and organization of the gardens fell to the lot of Enrique, who was quite content with the arrangement.

Eventually the ex-quartermaster suffered an apoplectic stroke and, once again, the position of head gardener fell vacant. The manager had also been changed, as the Colonel's accounts showed more imagination than accuracy, and a new manager arrived from the mainland to put things right. Signor Elias Montalban had been badly wounded as a Captain of Artillery during the battle for the Alcazar, and, invalided out of the army, had quickly found himself a useful job in hotel management. Being honest and intelligent, he now became the successful manager of the Isabella. His shrewd eye quickly appraised Enrique's exceptional ability and, after a short and informal interview, he appointed the dedicated young Mallorcan to be his head gardener.

Enrique could hardly believe his luck and soon moved his few belongings into the head gardener's cottage which, though but a larger and more picturesque version of his former garden shack, was to Enrique a palace. It seemed to him that he had reached the pinnacle of his career, and now he longed to share it with someone.

During the years just before the European War broke out, Enrique had become friendly with the only other person beside Manuel Salem whom he had allowed to be close to him. This was a severely wounded ex-fisherman, Carlos Ortega, who had joined the hotel as a trainee waiter when the Isabella reopened. Carlos' fortunes had risen almost in parallel with Enrique's own, until he became assistant head waiter at about the same time that Enrique was coming in line for the job of head gardener. Then

quite suddenly, just before the outbreak of the Second
World War, Carlos had become involved in some hotel
scandal and, without saying a word to anyone, had left
for the mainland.

Enrique was sad for his friend and also much troubled
by the thought that Carlos had left without saying goodbye,
but he was saddest of all because he had lost the one person
of his own age in whom he could confide his ambition to
find himself a wife.

The World War came, and Enrique continued to build
up the lovely gardens into a wonder of landscaping, filled
all the year round with flowers and evergreens, every
corner a surprise and a delight to the eye. There were few
foreign visitors to the Isabella during those war years but,
with Spain's carefully guarded neutrality, a new wealth
had come to her, for she was now courted by the major
powers and benefited from the peaceful prosperity which
started to grow with her non-involvement in the European
holocaust. Throughout the war years, the only signs of
battle around the Balearic Islands were seen in the badly-
damaged ships which sometimes limped into Palma Har-
bour, where Spanish neutrality, under international law,
permitted them to remain only long enough for essential
repairs to make them sea-worthy.

All through this time Enrique worked from sun-up to
sun-down, endlessly seeking to perfect his creation, and
his garden grew and matured until the scent of its flowers
surrounded the hotel with a sensual, almost palpable cloud.

When the war ended a new managing director came from
the mainland to take over and rebuild the Reina Isabella.
To Enrique's joy and astonishment, this important person-
age turned out to be the former assistant head waiter and
his long-lost friend, Carlos Ortega.

That the ex-fisherman had changed with the passing of
the years was obvious only to someone who had known
him well before he left the island, and quite apart from his

wealth and importance, Enrique knew at once that there
had been a big change in his friend's character. Although
they came into contact with each other almost immediately
in the way of business, Carlos showed none of the warmth
and companionship that he had once felt for his friend.

Enrique, being a man who understood from experience
what solitude meant, recognized this new characteristic in
his old friend, and, with the natural dignity of the Spanish
islander, did not attempt to break through the barrier of
reserve that Carlos had raised around himself.

By this time, Enrique, who was now forty, had made up
his mind to take a wife, and had, in his innocence of any
experience with women, fallen deeply in love with one of
the chambermaids at the Reina Elizabeth, as Don Carlos
had now renamed his beautifully rebuilt hotel.

Daniella Murmoz was only just out of her teens, and would
have been extremely pretty if it hadn't been for her teeth,
which were uneven and, like most of the islanders', sadly
neglected. She was the only child of an impoverished family
living in the district of Benisalem. Her father had died of
tuberculosis when she was a small child and, soon after, her
mother succumbed to a vicious dose of influenza, quickly
followed by double pneumonia. The orphaned Daniella
had a brief and desperately unhappy six months with an
alcoholic aunt, who regularly beat her when sober, and
tried to kill her when drunk. From this hell she had been
rescued by the parish priest, who firmly believed that the
aunt was possessed by the devil, and Daniella was admitted
to a nearby convent.

For a time the drunken aunt appeared outside the nunnery
and hurled curses indiscriminately at her niece, the priest
and the nuns, till one day she was knocked down and killed
by a passing lorry on its way to deliver alcohol – thus
confirming the parish priest's belief in divine mercy and
poetic justice.

Until she was sixteen, Daniella lived contentedly with

the strict but kindly nuns, who worked her hard and gave
her the rudiments of an education, the mortal fear of God,
and the acceptance of a life of servitude. When her seven-
teenth birthday came round, the nuns took her for an interview with the manager of the Reina Elizabeth, and Daniella
became a new addition to the hard-working staff of the
hotel.

Up until her induction into this exciting new life,
Daniella had never been to a cinema, nor read a book other
than the Holy Bible and the *Lives of the Saints* – but once she
had overcome the mortal fear that such deadly sins would
be punished instantly by the ever ready Hand of God, she
took to these pleasures like a duck to water. That hackneyed
simile is particularly apt in Daniella's case, because she
emerged slowly from being the epitome of the ugly, dowdy
duckling into a lovely swan – provided she didn't smile and
show her ugly teeth. Her face, from chubby, well-scrubbed
girlhood, developed into the classic lines of Spanish beauty
for which the island women, with their Moorish and Jewish
ancestry, are renowned. While her mouth remained closed
in an enigmatic smile, or her face was composed in the
serenity of sleep, Daniella Murmoz was beautiful – but
when she laughed, her uncared-for, crooked teeth spoilt the
promise of her lovely lips.

Perhaps it was this strange dichotomy that appealed so
much to Enrique, for his face had the tough, handsome
manliness that is summed up so aptly by the Spanish word
macho, while his twisted, humped body seemed to deny him
the further right to that term, and prevented him from being
a welcome *novio* to the island girls. In reality, it was Enrique's
self-imposed aloofness that formed the barrier between
himself and romantic love, for, though he did not know it,
the contrast of his good looks and crooked body made him
strangely attractive to the girls in the hotel, who were the
only women he ever came into contact with.

Of course he could have bought himself a Palma whore,

but Enrique had that deep puritanical streak which is sometimes the result of extreme hardship and suffering, and he
was a man of strong convictions and decided views. One of
these was that he wanted love – for himself, just as he was,
with all his ugliness and faults – not just purchased lust or
physical relief from a practised prostitute.

All his bottled-up passion had been channelled into
tending the ultra feminine glory of a garden. This, more
than anything else, had been the reason for his phenomenal
success as a gardener, but now that Enrique had reached
the pinnacle of his career, he was in a position to offer
security to a bride, and, at last, to be able to share his hoard
of love with another human being.

Daniella, too, desperately wanted the fulfilment of love,
but she could imagine it only in terms of her adored movies,
or as presented in the trashy fan magazines and dreadful
romantic novels which she devoured with hungry passion.
Each night she prayed to the Blessed Virgin to send her a
handsome lover. In the meantime, noticing Enrique's glowing eyes fixed upon her, wordlessly watching her every
move, she was both flattered and excited. Drawn by his
strangely attractive ugliness, she saw in him the embodi-
ment of Beauty and the Beast, and began to spin around him
a romantic web of fantasy, which to her meant love. Thus
their strange mating ritual commenced.

The other girls teased Daniella at first, jealous that the
head gardener, with his fine face and crooked body, had
not favoured them with his attentions, especially now that
his new-found happiness had given his stern features such
an appealing radiance.

Over the years, even when he had begun to earn a proper
salary, Enrique had always been frugal and, as he had
nothing but himself to spend it on, he had saved a respect-
able sum of money. This he now lavished on Daniella in
the form of frequent, enormous and garish boxes of
chocolates. Only when gorged to the point of nausea did

Daniella ask him to stop giving her them, and then Enrique bombarded her with flowers – the most beautiful, exotic and expensive of rare blooms.

Daniella, with her child-woman's mind full of images of screen romance and cheap novels, saw her suitor through a haze of glamour. With closed eyes, and her lovely body aflame, she imagined herself as the beautiful virgin, being carried off in the strong arms of the villainous hunch-back, who would suddenly be turned into the handsome prince that he really was by the power and purity of her love.

The convent-bred girl suffered as acutely from her perfectly natural longings and her carefully implanted religious fears and prejudices as she did from her awareness of the marring effect on her beauty of her ugly teeth. One of the young maids, a friend of Daniella's, who had broken her front teeth in a motorcycle accident while riding pillion, used the insurance money paid up by the guilty party – a drunken driver – to have the damage repaired by a Palma dental surgeon, and the result had been successful enough to rouse envious longings in Daniella for the same miraculous operation. When she found out how much it had cost her friend, she had been plunged into despair, for although up to then she had accepted the fact of her ugly teeth, to have the solution in sight and then realize that it was beyond her grasp was too much to bear.

Enrique had found her weeping alone in the garden, and when he had tried to comfort her with the gift of a rare potted plant, Daniella had hurled it to the ground and then, appalled at what she had done, had collapsed in hysterics in Enrique's arms. All reserve gone, the poor girl poured out her new hopes and sudden despair, and quite suddenly Enrique saw the perfect way to prove his love and make her happy ever after. He would pay for this wonderful doctor to perform the miraculous operation! No matter what it cost, he would pay for it, somehow!

Daniella stopped crying and burst into radiant if rather

ugly smiles. This was indeed true love! This was real
happiness! This was the way it happened in the movies!
Her arms were round Enrique's body in a moment, and hot
passionate kisses were rained on his lips till he, too, was
caught up in the whirlwind of her happiness.

So Enrique drew out a large part of his savings from the
bank, and Daniella went to Palma to be examined by the
expensive miracle-worker in reconstructive dental surgery.

To give Dr Alfredo Montseguro his due, he certainly
made a marvellous job of Daniella's teeth. Every week she
took the bus into Palma to spend a painful hour at a time
in the chair, while the skilled fingers of her dental surgeon
drilled and capped, extracted, and reshaped her over-
crowded mouth, till one day she returned to the hotel with
a numb but shining face and a temporary set of top front
teeth to show for her pains. She ran directly to find Enrique
and show him the first-fruits of Dr Montseguro's labour
and, of course, Enrique was beside himself with joy to see
her so happy.

Slowly, week after week, the extraordinary change took
place, till three months after those first radical extractions,
Daniella's teeth were as perfect as the rest of her beautiful
features – as crowning a glory as her shining hair. She took
the bus back to the hotel, unable to resist smiling all the
way, watched in open admiration by the male passengers,
and ill-concealed envy by the female ones.

The new, glowingly lovely Daniella naturally rushed to
show Enrique – who, for the first time, felt the cold hand
of dread touch his generous heart when he saw the incredible transformation. His spirit seemed to shrivel within
him and he gasped with the sudden pain of it, for, at that
moment, as Daniella stood there pirouetting and smiling
her dazzling new smile, Enrique knew that he must lose
her – for what chance would his twisted body have against
the handsome perfection that surely must be the shape of
her future suitors?

Daniella was far too carried away by the dizzy excitement of being her new self to notice and, after kissing Enrique warmly but without passion – and with considerable care not to loosen her new teeth before they had finally set in her mouth – she rushed back to the hotel to show all her friends how beautiful she was.

For Enrique it was pure horror! Although he was normally a tough and phlegmatic man, of strong but rigidly controlled emotions, he was, by his very nature, the gentlest of souls, and the sudden fiery furnace of jealousy that burned in him day and night was as foreign to him as the thought of violence or murder. Dreading that he would alienate Daniella, he tried to avoid her, but instead found himself constantly watching her.

Their break-up was as inevitable as it was agonizing to Enrique. Daniella seemed obsessed by her new-found power over men and flirted as openly as she dared. Her convent training still held her back from actually giving herself to a man outside the marriage bed, but she became coquettish to a degree that would have been unthinkable for her before the miraculous transformation.

Don Carlos Ortega himself wasn't slow to notice the change, for his sharp eyes were always scanning his hotel staff for any signs of slackness or discord which might affect the smooth running of the Reina Elizabeth, and he would certainly have intervened in this potentially explosive situation had not Fate taken a hand in it first.

An American film executive had arrived at the hotel, on the look-out for further locations for a film which was being made in Spain. This tough, dynamic young man had about him the confident air of one who could handle any situation – especially (and here his athletic good looks emphasized the point) any situation involving women. Already his bright blue, slightly short-sighted eyes and his close-cut curly blond hair had caused something of a stir among the island girls working at the hotel, for Tom

Marchant was *macho* in a thoroughly Anglo-Saxon way –
and he knew it.

Daniella's excitement was obvious. In the Americano
she saw the chance of a lifetime; it was just the kind of
situation she had read about so often in the cheap movie fan
magazines which were the inspiration of her waking and
sleeping fantasies. She saw herself being asked to fly with
him to Hollywood for a screen test which would make her
the discovery of the Movie Capital, and lead her to fame
and riches as the Spanish Marilyn Monroe.

And this indeed was what the American proposed soon
after he seduced her on the front seat of a hired car within
a week of his arrival. Skilled in love making, he carried
Daniella along with his lust until she panted for him to
take her. When he did so, he was amazed at the emotions
she roused in him. Sexually jaded from too many encounters
with worldly and .ambitious would-be actresses, he
found Daniella's fresh and innocent response a revelation.
Alternately laughing and crying with the intensity of her
newly-awakened passion, the beautiful Spanish girl finally
lay back exhausted in his arms, and the American knew that
he had found something too precious to throw aside lightly.

Tom Marchant was a man who made his decisions
quickly, and then kept to them, and he realized that Daniella
would make him a perfect mistress – someone he could
enjoy and, at the same time, mould in a way that would
bring him credit in his career. Perhaps he would even marry
her and make her Mrs Tom Marchant – number three. The
following day – twenty-four hours before he was due to fly
back to Madrid – he asked Daniella to go with him.

Daniella was overwhelmed by the sheer wonder of it all.
Her feeble objections – the last vestiges of her convent
upbringing – soon gave way, and she accepted his offer
with the same blissful, artless readiness with which she had
given herself. Any thoughts of Enrique, and the fact that
he had made all this possible, were swept away in the

marvel of the imminent fulfilment of her dreams, and then and there in the American's room she threw away any remaining caution, and they both lustily satisfied their passions, to seal the bargain.

There was no reason to delay the elopement, for the girl had no one to tell or seek permission from – new clothes could be bought in Madrid, and the American had already thoughtfully provided her with a travelling wardrobe, purchased that morning in Palma. And so Daniella left the Reina Elizabeth, with only one close friend guessing at the truth of what was happening.

She had one moment of misgiving as they waited impatiently to board the plane at Palma Airport, when quite suddenly Enrique came into her mind and she felt a sharp pang of conscience. In a spontaneous outburst she told the American all about her teeth, and Enrique's kindness in providing the money for the transformation. The shrewd young man instantly saw that she was genuinely fond of her benefactor – and realized that here was a good opportunity to shine in her eyes – so he promptly offered to send back to Enrique the whole sum as soon as they reached Madrid, and as proof of his sincerity he took out two policies from the automatic insurance dispensing machine, and made them out in favour of Enrique.

Daniella was overjoyed at this apparently generous gesture on the part of her lover, and clung to Marchant like one of Enrique's vines. Twenty minutes later they had boarded the aircraft and the powerful Tripulacion was swinging down the runway and lifting off into the lowering cloud base above.

Another fifteen minutes, and Daniella was enjoying more new experiences – her first flight in an aircraft and her first bottle of champagne. Fifteen minutes more, and the tail-mounted jet engine failed, necessitating a diversion to Barcelona Airport. Precisely thirty minutes after take-off, the airliner, with yet another engine failing, slammed into a mist-enshrouded mountainside.

There were of course no survivors. The next day the manager of Palma Airport telephoned Don Carlos to say that two of his guests – they had listed their addresses as that of the hotel when buying the airline tickets – had been passengers on the flight which had ended so tragically – a Mr Tom Marchant and a Señorita Daniella Murmoz. It was then that Carlos Ortega decided, in view of his earlier friendship with Enrique Inca, to break the news personally to his head gardener.

No one knows what went on inside the gardener's cottage, but Don Carlos did not emerge until twelve hours after he had entered it, bearing a large bottle of Cognac.

Enrique was back at work in the gardens on the following day, but had become, understandably, totally uncommunicative, and remained so for several weeks, toiling grimly from sunrise to sunset, eating little and speaking to no one.

A month or so later, an insurance representative came to see Don Carlos, and asked for his assistance in a matter of business.

'Señor Enrique Inca is the beneficiary of two insurance policies for the substantial sum of 1,000,000 pesetas each, being the sums insured by Mr Tom Marchant and Señorita Daniella Murmoz, in his name. The company has written several letters to the beneficiary, but he has not replied. As Señor Inca is your gardener, Don Carlos, perhaps you know whether the problem is that he cannot read or write?'

Don Carlos replied gravely that this was not the case, but that Señor Inca's grief at the loss of his two close friends had made him almost a recluse; and that it would be best for the insurance company to let him handle the situation. The insurance assessor willingly left the matter in Don Carlos' capable hands, having received a receipt from him for the custody of the cheque, and, after carefully considering the implications, the hotel manager made his way once more to Enrique Inca's cottage.

It took him a long time to persuade Enrique that it had
been Daniella's intention to send for him as soon as she
became successful in the movies. The cheque, when he
produced it, was what finally convinced Enrique of his lost
love's good faith. Twelve hours and a bottle of Don Carlos'
best brandy later, Enrique had accepted both the cheque and
Don Carlos' advice to invest it in a small horticultural
business of his own. It was thus that Daniella Gardens came
into being, and Enrique eventually made his well-deserved
fortune.

One point continued to bother Don Carlos, who had a
methodical mind: how was the insurance company able to
identify the remains of Daniella Murmoz and others in the
appalling wreckage which had been so graphically depicted
in the newspapers?

Dr Montseguro eventually furnished him with the answer
when they met on the occasion of a dentists' conference,
held at the Reina Elizabeth, some time later. They had been
chatting respectfully about the tragic business of Daniella's
death and the dental surgeon had added his condolences on
the sad loss to the hotel of such a beautiful girl.

'Yes,' he said gloomily, 'I read her name on the passenger
list published in the newspaper, and rang up the airline to
offer my services for identification purposes. It was the
least I could do, as the señorita had been such a splendid
patient.

'In this sort of accident, identification is usually very
difficult, but in Señorita Murmoz's case it was simple. I
instantly recognized my handiwork from photographs of
the jaws and, in her case, it made all the difference.'

A Question of Time

I QUITE APPRECIATE your position, sir. The Press have been particularly difficult over the recent figures for violent crime, and obviously you are under pressure from the Home Secretary. But you, above all, sir, will appreciate *our* position.

The whole country's police forces are well below strength, what with one budget after another whittling us down to the bare minimum required to maintain law and order, particularly, in the Metropolitan area where, as you yourself well know, sir, we are stretched to our operational limit.

The number of unsolved violent crimes, with particular emphasis on murder, has become unacceptable, and we are all backing you to the hilt in your fight for higher figures in police recruitment and more technical facilities to back us up.

However, with respect to the unsolved crime that the Press seem to have chosen as their main target in the present smear campaign, I assure you, sir, that there is a perfectly valid reason for our having been unable to present a case

to the Director of Public Prosecutions. If only we had more
time we could wrap up this case, with a watertight certainty of a successful prosecution.

Perhaps, if I just went over the outstanding points in
this murder, I could give you a better idea of our present
situation.

You will remember, sir, that the murder victim, Dr Roger
Scarsdale, a well-respected scholar in his own specialized
field of research, was found stabbed to death early in the
morning of September 5th on the Embankment near
Whitefriars.

The cause of death was, according to our Forensic
Department, a single powerful blow to the heart by a
narrow-bladed weapon, bringing about almost instantaneous death. The Coroner pointed out at the inquest that
the blow had been delivered by someone facing the deceased, and either with great skill and knowledge of the
use of the weapon or by a lucky blow – that is, of course,
lucky from the point of view of the assailant.

There was no sign of a struggle and, as nothing appears
to be missing from the personal possessions of the deceased,
we have discounted robbery as the motive for the crime.

Three possibilities remained. One, that the victim was
attacked by some person under the influence of a deeply
disturbing narcotic drug, such as mescaline. Two, that Dr
Scarsdale was murdered by a maniac, for no other reason
than the deranged person's desire to kill. Three, that the
deceased was the victim of someone who bore him a grudge.

Of the three possibilities, the first seemed unlikely, as
only one blow was struck and normally – if you'll forgive
the use of that word in these circumstances – normally a
series of blows, struck indiscriminately, would be a more
likely pattern for a crime committed by a violently disturbed person.

The same sort of argument presented itself in the second
possibility – murder by a maniac – because, like murders

committed under the influence of drugs, most maniacal killings – such as those of Jack the Ripper or his latter day counterpart, Haigh, bear the mark of sub-bestial savagery in the subsequent mutilation of the corpse.

My colleagues agreed with me that the third possibility – a killing with revenge as the motive – seemed to be the most likely.

Naturally the case required a complete and thorough investigation, so we started off with a careful screening of all information that we could obtain on Dr Scarsdale's background – and an interesting fact emerged.

Nowhere could our investigating team come up with the smallest clue, or the slightest evidence of the murder victim's involvement in any scandal or sexual entanglement with any person, female or male, or any misdemeanour, in either business or social life, which would have provided a motive for murder.

The deceased's private life seems to have been blameless and his public one was a model of discreet self-effacement, to the point of anonymity – as I have found is often the case with distinguished scholars who usually only emerge into the spotlight of publicity when they receive some outstanding award or public honour.

Dr Scarsdale was just over thirty-six years old when he was murdered and, therefore, might be considered to have reached the pinnacle of his well-established career.

However, there was one point that arose during our investigative procedure that I feel had some considerable significance. While going through some of the scientific papers and articles that he had written, I found something that might have had a bearing on the one motive that we considered feasible: that of jealousy or bitter resentment, which, in my experience as a police officer in the last twenty-five years, I have found to be quite common in violent crimes.

The paper to which I refer was the verbatim account of

a lecture which Dr Scarsdale had delivered at the Royal
Institution in the spring of the year in which the murder
was committed. During the course of this lecture he had
referred, obliquely at first and then more directly as the
lecture proceeded, to the work of a colleague of his who,
in his considered and expert opinion, had, in his researches,
based a number of vitally important assumptions on what
Dr Scarsdale believed to be wholly unstable evidence which
he felt certain he could prove to be erroneous.

Furthermore, he named the misguided fellow-scholar,
and, though he referred to the past achievements of this
colleague with respect, it was clear that he now placed
precious little academic value on the results of his colleague's
work.

Now that might not strike you, sir, as much of a motive
for murder, but I have on occasion, in the course of my
duties, come across a number of academic persons, and
some of them seemed to me to be particularly spiteful and
vindictive where rival scholars in their own particular field
of research were concerned.

Be that as it may, in the case of Dr Scarsdale there seemed
to be a distinct possibility that such a motive might apply
to the object of his scathing attack. With this in mind I
located the academic in question – a Dr Gareth Carrington
– an older and equally highly-respected scholar, who had
been acknowledged, up to the time of Scarsdale's lecture,
as one of the world experts in their mutual field of research
and was, in fact, on the point of retiring with an assured
honour.

The furore in the academic world that followed Dr
Scarsdale's lecture made little public impact, but in the
restricted circle of scholars and students of this highly
specialized field of research there was considerable con-
troversy and excitement. The subject under scrutiny was
the study of edged weapons.

Our own Forensic Department at Nottingham possesses

all the important works on this subject and I understand
that Dr Carrington has appeared as an expert witness on
occasion – both for the Crown and the Defence. Dr Harold,
one of our forensic boffins, whose speciality is firearms and
forensic ballistics, holds a high opinion of Dr Carrington's
paper on edged weapons and their history.

My own interviews with Dr Carrington aroused my
suspicions, for he proved to be a somewhat cynical man,
who obviously didn't relish having his work questioned
and who, while outwardly sympathizing with the relatives
of the deceased, equally obviously did not hold much
personal regard for Dr Scarsdale's achievements in this
field. 'Too young and too inexperienced,' I think were the
words he used to describe his detractor – for to a scholar
of Dr Carrington's forty years' standing Dr Scarsdale's
mere sixteen years' study of edged weapons seemed to be
somewhat inadequate.

Moreover, a number of circumstances seemed to point
to more than just the remote possibility of Dr Carrington's
involvement in the crime. One of these was a quickly-
controlled display of temper in my presence, when he
was referring to Scarsdale's own work – 'plagiarism' was
one word that he used.

As to the other circumstances, they were quite interesting
enough to warrant further investigation.

First, Dr Carrington had been working not too far from
the Embankment, at Whitefriars, on the day before the
murder – the time of which the Forensic Department has
pinpointed as being approximately midnight. Second, it is
highly likely that Dr Scarsdale knew the identity of his
assailant, in view of the absence of any struggle. Third, the
Coroner's remarks regarding the expert way in which the
weapon had been used in striking the fatal blow, leads one
to conjecture that the assailant could quite possibly have
known as much about edged weapons as Dr Scarsdale did.

Certainly I felt that I had now established a motive and

prepared a case of which I would have been quite confident, had we eventually taken it to the Director of Public Prosecutions. However, as with most murders involving the use of a deadly weapon, the vital piece of evidence would rest with the expert opinion of the Forensic Department – based on long and exhaustive tests carried out over quite a considerable period of time.

As you know, sir, the shape and depth of a fatal wound can be matched to a possible weapon by using an animal carcase as the recipient of similar blows with a suspected weapon and taking plaster casts of the resulting wound, which then can be compared with casts of the original wound. Bloodstain tests can be checked on the comparison microscope and the observation of various other complex chemical reactions are another part of this kind of forensic investigation.

We enlisted the aid of the Metropolitan Police River Division, and dragged the whole area at high tide, while at low tide we examined every foot of the foreshore for several hundred yards on either side of the site of the murder. Uniformed police minutely searched the whole area around Whitefriars and the Embankment, without coming up with anything remotely resembling the murder weapon. Although several edged weapons in various states of preservation were dredged up from the river bed with magnetic grapnels, all were discarded as being inapplicable to the type of wound inflicted.

So there the whole matter rests. I know the Home Secretary was an acquaintance of Dr Scarsdale. I understand that they were members of the same club, and, naturally, he has taken a personal interest in the case.

As I explained to you, sir, the whole prosecution is going to rest on conclusive forensic evidence – plus, of course, the careful build-up by the D.P.P. of the circumstantial evidence. Notwithstanding the Coroner's statements about the expert use of the murder weapon and the academic feud that existed between the two scholars, there is still insufficient concrete evidence to bring about a conviction, unless the Forensic Department weighs in with some convincing proof.

All my instincts tell me that Dr Carrington is the murderer. He has no real alibi, apart from being seen at his club at a somewhat earlier hour than that fixed for the murder, so he would have had ample time to get to White-friars from there even if he had walked. Whether he persuaded Dr Scarsdale to meet him on the Embankment at such an unusually late hour, or whether he knew that it was Scarsdale's habit to take a stroll along the Embankment after having left the Mermaid Theatre – which we know, he regularly patronized on the same night of each month – is a matter for conjecture.

There we have it, sir – motive, opportunity, even a probable scenario of the crime and, above all, the ability to deliver the skilled fatal blow. But without that damned weapon, we are quite helpless to proceed further. The Defence would see us off on the circumstantial evidence alone.

However, I'm pretty certain where the murder weapon is located at this moment. Cleaned and replaced in its usual position, among thousands of such weapons, in the largest and most comprehensive collection of this kind found in the world – a place where both Scarsdale and Carrington would have been familiar figures in the normal course of their research.

I refer, sir, to the Edged Weapons collection in the Tower of London, which is only a mile or so from White-friars. At the most conservative estimate it must contain several thousand examples of the sort of weapon that we are looking for. The tests on a murder weapon of this type take at least three or four days of painstaking work to make absolutely certain that all the relevant experts agree.

So as you can see, sir – it is only a question of time!

House-proud

As SOON AS they saw the house, the Bartletts knew that their five-year-long search was over. If ever the great architect and philosopher, Vitruvius, could have transmuted 'The Golden Mien' into the form of a twentieth-century house, then this perfect example of an architect's skill would have been the epitome of that master craftsman's teaching – that the 'golden section' is governed by the mystical 'canon'.

'It's going to be our pride and joy,' smiled Gail Bartlett, not very originally, as she affectionately squeezed her husband's arm.

'Almost too good to be true,' mused John Bartlett, equally unoriginally, for, being an architect and interior designer himself, he knew that until a full structural survey had been carried out, the probable and improbable snags would not come to light.

'Oh come now, darling, you're just being over-cautious,' encouraged his beautiful wife, and John Bartlett had to agree that Gail's instincts were usually right, and in this case her insistence on seeing this particular house before

they went back to Los Angeles seemed to have been
inspired.

When they had first seen the house, as they drove round
the shielding screen of tall yew trees which bordered the
sweeping approach of the gravelled drive, their immediate
impression was almost as though they had both received
an electric shock.

Both of them later admitted to a feeling of déjà-vu when
they had completed their thorough and increasingly delighted inspection of the interior – from the fine oak-
panelled hall, with its imposing minstrels' gallery, through
the large drawing-room, lit by generous airy windows and
obviously warmed by the roomy sit-round fireplace, right
up to the long attic studio room that ran the entire length
of the house. Every room seemed to be a revelation – never
exactly what they had expected, but always, somehow,
marvellously familiar.

John explained it: 'It's the sheer proportion of it all –
everything fits into a perfectly conceived pattern of different
shapes and sizes – so that you are only aware that it all
adds up to a beautiful house – or, if you prefer it, a beautiful
home. We've never lived in anything like this before and
yet we seem to have lived here always.'

Their minds were made up. The local solicitor, Ben
Waters, of Waters, Chambers, Monkton and Todd, amiably
and efficiently completed the deals, escrow and deeds, with
their Los Angeles lawyer, Martin Bentley, of Bentley,
Johnson and Merriweather – and, as far as either lawyer
could see, there were no major snags in the title deeds and,
therefore, no reason for delay in signing the contracts.

Five weeks to the day after their preliminary inspection
of the house, the property became theirs, and two weeks
later the Bartletts began that normally infuriating and ex-
hausting business of 'moving in'. Two large pantechnicons
transported their furniture, glass, china and carpets, linen
and pictures, in one quick and efficient move, and, to

everyone's surprise, everything seemed to fit in place, as though the Bartletts were coming *back* home, instead of moving into a new house. Even the tough, cynical old foreman, who must have moved thousands of people's belongings in his time, said that he'd never seen an easier move into a lovelier home.

'Goddammit,' said Gail's husband, 'I was dreading this part of it, but it's all been so easy – just as if the house were expecting us! Darling, *we're home!*'

The same sentiment was echoed, in various different ways, by the fifty or so guests who made up the Bartletts' housewarming party: it was a huge success! Everyone seemed genuinely delighted with the house and some were more than envious – in fact, both Gail and John received broad hints that, if they should sell at some future date, a willing buyer would show them a handsome profit, any time!

All this naturally tended to leave the Bartletts with an even stronger conviction that they had stumbled across the bargain of their lives, and it was then that I came into the picture.

My name is Henry Marchant and I have known John Bartlett since school-days and Gail since their engagement party. As I haven't been fortunate enough to have found anyone like John's wife, so far, I am a confirmed bachelor – though by no means a lonely one! Gail, with that odd match-making inclination that a happily-married woman often falls prey to, is always getting me to meet various attractive unattached friends.

I had missed the houseparty as, at the time, I was away in Europe, and when I returned to Los Angeles I found the invitation among my mail. I rang John up to apologize for missing the housewarming, and was immediately invited down for the weekend.

The house lay well back from a long side road, which meandered picturesquely along a twisting valley that ran for some two miles off the side of the Pacific Highway. The beautiful building was finally approached by a fully-matured yew-tree-lined drive, which was further ennobled by a fine pair of wrought iron gates, set between grey stone portals, one of which bore a well-polished bronze plaque on which the name 'Asgaard' stood out in low relief.

When I drew up outside the Ionic-pillared portico I had an indefinable feeling that I had arrived at somewhere important. Without knowing anything about the place – without it being in the least flamboyant – I felt that it was somehow *significant*.

The weekend was a happy one, as I had expected with two such joyous people, and I certainly agreed with them that their new home was exceptional. I felt particularly delighted with their choice because I am very fond of them both, and I've always felt that, had I met someone as lovely as the slim, dark-brunette, gentle Gail, with those haunting grey-green eyes and that marvellously companionable personality, I would have asked her to marry me on the spot. John I had always considered as a brother, in a way replacing but not supplanting the brother that I had lost in the war. These two fine people made the times we spent together some of the happiest of my life.

On the Sunday morning when we met at breakfast in the sun-warmed dining-room, John asked me if I could help him find a spot to sink a well. Now, John is an architect, whereas I am a structural engineer – or in lay terms, a builder – and from time to time we have co-operated on various successful projects. During the course of one of these we had run into a water problem for a large garden, and I had then, somewhat shyly, confessed to him that I was a 'water witch'.

Of course, the real name for this ability to find water is 'dowsing', and the term – which means 'searching for' – covers a multitude of subjects, from finding running water in pipes, springs, sources and underground streams to locating current moving along buried electric cables, or gas passing through sunken pipes – in fact, to pinpointing the position of practically any form of subterranean energy.

This ability, which I believe we all have to some degree, is probably a relic of the survival mechanism of our remote ancestors. I have had it since a favourite and decidedly eccentric uncle showed me how to dowse when I was a boy, and I've even been able to find underground caves, tunnels and collapsed mine shafts by using one of the many aids to dowsing such as twigs, pendulums or angled rods. The latter I have often made up, on the spot, out of cut and bent wire coat-hangers, and I find them just as effective as the more usual 'L'-shaped copper wire rods that I habitually carry in my car.

These I brought out at John's request, and before lunch I had quartered the large lawn that dominated the south side of the property and, watched by an amused and interested Gail, I had found a surprisingly strong spring a few yards from a circular clump of fine yew-trees, almost next to the gates.

There, sixty feet below me (I used a method called the Bishop's Rule which I won't go into here), I knew that they would find a good flow – about fifty gallons an hour – of pure spring water, perfectly adequate for watering the garden, and a marvellous bonus as drinking water – something that only people who habitually drink spring water will know.

Contemporary science is still chary of accepting dowsing as a valid, empirically-based phenomenon, but I have found it one hundred per cent reliable. I was therefore elated at having located a good source of spring water for my friends, but at the same time I suddenly found myself feeling uneasy about their beautiful new acquisition. When I had arrived at the house on that bright, late fall morning, and even during the enthusiastic guided tour I received from the two people I loved most on this earth, I had had no feelings whatsoever, apart from a delighted wonder that such a bargain should have fallen into such deserving hands. Then, while dowsing the grounds for water, a feeling of momentary unease had come over me – 'someone stepping on one's grave' is the expression that best describes the sensation.

I have given only a very simple explanation of dowsing – naturally, the whole business is far more complex as it is a part of man's overall sensitivity. And quite distinctly, I had picked up – dowsed, or whatever other word you choose to describe the sensation – a feeling of menace, a foreboding, a shadow of impending chaos in this environment of order, peace and serenity. Moreover, the feeling wouldn't respond to reason and go away, and I found myself wondering whether I should try to explain it to my friends, or just ignore it for the time being and then, perhaps at some later date, pass on to them the nagging doubt that had beset me.

Because of our close friendship, John must have sensed that something was amiss, and later that evening, while we were drinking some of his excellent brandy, he suddenly asked me, point blank, if I had any reservations about the place.

I hedged a bit, but eventually I saw that I had no alternative but to 'come clean'. 'Frankly, John,' I said, at last, 'I don't know about you, but I find the whole deal too satisfactory by half! If this property was as desirable as it appears to be, how come the last owners parted with it for such a reasonable price as you tell me you paid for it? You and I have been in the construction business for a long time. Do you ever recall finding such a bargain for one of our clients? If the house and grounds had been in a badly run-down state, it would still have been a very reasonable price for it all, but, like this – sure as Hell! – it's a give-away – a steal!'

John agreed, and then gave me some interesting information: 'The death of the previous owner, an old lady who

died quite suddenly, leaving the property to her sole heir –
a nephew – brought the house on to the market, and we
were only the second lot of people to see over it. Apparently
it didn't suit the first prospective client because he was a
property developer, and we're in a restricted area as far as
any further development is concerned.'

'And you found that the price was too good to refuse?'
I queried, almost as a statement of fact.

'Precisely! well, as you know, Henry, we'd been looking
for a house for four years or so, and we don't want to wait
too much longer before starting a family. Frankly, can you
think of a better place to raise children than here?'

'No, I must agree with you, John, that room at the top
is just about perfect for a nursery – especially if you're
thinking of a large family!'

'I know large families are out of vogue, but Gail and I
have always hankered after one and, somehow, this place
just seems to be made for kids – all I know is that I would
have loved it as a kid myself!'

So the conversation continued in this happy, constructive
vein for the rest of the evening, with the three of us
swapping reminiscences of our childhood – and with those
memories still lighting our thoughts, we yawned ourselves
to our late beds.

In the morning I had to leave early for the city, but John
had already moved his drawing-office equipment into one
of the north-facing upstairs bedrooms – a lovely, light, airy
place – with a magnificent view over the valley below.
This steep cleft in the hills surrounding the house, which
was built on the summit of a plateau, started the downward
sweep of its lightly-wooded sides within twenty yards of
the rear of the house. There was just sufficient room for a
long, narrow patio, paved with good stone flags and edged
with protective walls made of large, tumbled rocks that
looked as though they might, originally, have been part of
some ancient neolithic stone circle.

On the way back to Los Angeles I found myself musing about the odd feeling which I had experienced the day before when I was dowsing for the spring, but, eventually, I put it out of my mind – and I would probably have forgotten it, but for a chance meeting with an old friend from my Rhodes Scholarship days at Oxford.

Roger Mellows was a natural scholar of the highways and byways of human behaviour, a fine academic who could have held the chair of history at pretty well any university in the world. An accomplished linguist, as well as being an historian of note, Roger had returned to Oxford on a foundation grant, to study the same subject that I was reading, classical architecture. I owe my sound grounding in that most beautiful of studies more to this good friend than to my tutor who, although brilliant, lacked Roger's marvellous gift for enthusiastically communicating knowledge.

Roger's father was an eminent architect and a contemporary of Lutyens, the great Edwardian, whose elegant British country houses graced suitably lovely sites around the coast of that marvellous island, and whose great viceroy's palace in Delhi was one of the last vigorous manifestations of the dying British Empire. Like Lutyens, the elder Mellows had been a close friend of Rudyard Kipling, and had, on occasion, been a privileged listener, over the dinner-table, to the conversations between these two men.

Both of them were fascinated by the mystical side of architecture, and Lutyens had instructed Kipling in the finer points of the analysis and meaning of the architectural features of the great British cathedrals. 'Sermons in stone', he called them, and brilliantly brought them to life with his lucid explanations and beautifully graphic drawings, which he jotted down in an old exercise book that Kipling provided.

All this may seem irrelevant to my meeting with Roger Mellows and the strange events which succeeded it, but it gives some idea of the area of thought that we fell into during our impromptu reunion dinner. Over the brandy, at our club, I told Roger something of John Bartlett's proud new acquisition and then, oddly enough, of my own strange feeling of approaching chaos and disaster, and Roger became quite excited about it.

'Do you remember, Henry, reading a little book I lent you – years ago – by Claude Bragdon? It was called *The Beautiful Necessity*?'

'I do indeed,' I replied. 'A remarkable work, by someone who really understood what went on in the minds of the great architects, like Vitruvius, Palladio and Wren.'

'Well, Bragdon was a theosophist and a good mathematician, and he became quite an authority on projective geometry – not the highly academic stuff, but the down-to-earth projection of form and shape. He wrote other books on this subject, each equally fascinating – in fact I've been a fan of his work for years.'

'What are you leading up to?' I asked curiously.

'Bragdon had an ardent disciple, whom he himself probably didn't know well, but whom I got to know when I became involved in a series of lectures, given at Yale, on the concept of classical architecture in sacred buildings. One of the lectures I gave contained quite a lengthy reference to Bragdon's theory that "the beautiful necessity" was a means to encapsulate the ability of man to project, by form and shape, a field of force which would affect the immediate environment for the benefit of posterity. I called the lecture "Buildings for the future", and it was quite a success.

'Anyhow, this chap – Paul Harrington was his name – came up afterwards, full of congratulations, and was obviously anxious to pursue the subject further. He was a strange bird – a bit off-putting in a way – but he certainly was an enthusiast. An amateur architect himself, and a good one at that, he was a devoted admirer of Lutyens as well as Bragdon. It was more because of my father's association

with those two architects than for any real liking for
Harrington that I allowed a relationship to grow up between us.

'He was a most interesting scholar, of a number of
subjects, and, being independently wealthy, had been able
to pursue his studies without much difficulty. He was quite
a student of the more exotic religions, too, and he had gone
into ritual magic pretty thoroughly. But although he was
an intriguing acquaintance and I enjoyed his company on
an intellectual level, I never really warmed to the man. He
was too much of an eccentric and lived alone in a fine house,
which he had designed and built himself, somewhere up
near Carmel, just off the Pacific Highway. When you were
describing this house of John Bartlett's, it rang a bell –
perhaps you could do a rough sketch of the place?'

Fascinated by this turn of the conversation, I rapidly
complied and came up with a fair representation of the
house in elevation, a rough plan, and a site drawing from
my fairly accurate memory.

'That's it!' cried Roger excitedly. 'Well, I'm damned!
That's the place that Harrington showed me pictures of –
I remember the excellent plans which he had drawn as
though it were yesterday – what a bloody strange thing!
Your chum having bought Paul Harrington's home – it's
downright weird!

'Harrington lived alone, but he had a whole series of
housekeepers whom I'm sure he worked half to death,
keeping the place as spick and span as his pernickety soul
demanded. He told me himself that he couldn't keep
servants – even the local gardeners only worked for him
for a time, and then chucked their hand in. I can understand
it: he was a perfectionist to end all perfectionists – his
drawings conveyed that much – they really were beautifully
laid out, a superb piece of craftsmanship, and yet, in a
strange way – like Harrington himself – curiously imper-
sonal, as though there wasn't a real person inside the

elegant, cultured façade that he presented to the world. Do you know, he never once shook hands with me, or anyone else whom I can remember him meeting! Some fad he had about cleanliness being next to godliness – a queer cove altogether, probably in more ways than one, if the rumour was true.'

'What rumour?' I automatically asked.

'It was said, and probably with good reason, that Paul Harrington wanted to be associated always with his perfect home – and that he had designed, and executed in the strictest secrecy, an octagonal underground chamber, cut into the living rock, below the foundation of his house. It was a tomb, a mausoleum, in which – so the story goes – he was buried – embalmed – sitting upright in a great wooden chair, facing the rising sun! How's that for an odd bit of gossip? Perhaps that's what you picked up when you were dowsing for the well.'

Roger and I had often talked about the para-normal, and his curious story disturbed me considerably. Naturally, I did not pass the story on to John. I had no intention of raising a spectre in their long sought-for, new-found home. So there the whole matter would have ended as far as I was concerned, but for my next meeting with John, which was nothing if not traumatic.

The plain fact is that I hardly recognized him. John had grown a beard, which made him look ten years older, and in the six months since I had last seen him he had lost so much weight that he looked gaunt and haggard, in contrast to his normal trimly athletic self. When he spotted me in the smoking room of the club, where I had been hardly even a casual visitor for the previous six months, he seemed overjoyed, and immediately suggested that we should adjourn, after lunch, to my apartment and have a long talk together.

Lunch was a tense and unenjoyable affair, with John trying to make small talk, and then lapsing into a most uncharacteristic silence, while I deliberately chattered on in an attempt to keep the atmosphere cheerful, so that it was with a deeply felt sigh of relief that I followed him into my duplex apartment just off Laurel Canyon, and settled him into a comfortable chair with a stiff Remy Martin warming in his hand.

I didn't need the crystal ball of my balloon-glass to mist over to sense that John was going to tell me something about the house, but I was not prepared for the extraordinarily horrific tale that he told me on that afternoon.

Our last conversation of six months back had been about Gail, and their plans for starting a family, and indeed a month or so after my visit she had become pregnant. My friends' joy was complete when their doctor gave them the good news, and John became the happiest of expectant fathers – yet, within a few weeks, it became obvious that Gail wasn't enjoying her long-awaited pregnancy. It wasn't the to-be-expected early morning sickness, or stomach upsets and heartburn, which are, according to my married sister and various divorcee girlfriends, the common lot of most first pregnancies, but something far more disturbing.

Gail began to have a feeling of unease about the house – something like the first disturbing thoughts which I had experienced while dowsing the grounds. In the first few weeks of their move into the new house, she had had an almost fanatical desire to get everything straight, and then to keep it all as spick and span as she could – polishing the long heavy oaken bannisters and balustrades of the sweeping staircase and the minstrels' gallery, and even climbing up to wash the large chandelier – part of the magnificent fixtures that came with the house – until that impressive mass of glittering cut crystal sparkled like some vast dowager's giant diamond necklace. She waxed the panelling in the hall, dining-room and library until it reflected back the lights like dark wooden mirrors.

'Gail always seemed so intensely happy – busy all day

long about the house,' said John in bewilderment. 'I was delighted, of course, that she had taken such a shine – oh, Jesus! I didn't mean the pun! – I meant an almost *fanatical* interest in our home – when, in the Los Angeles apartment, she'd only done whatever basic housework was strictly necessary – but then I put it all down to the fact that now we had a *real* home – not just a rented apartment, but a magnificent place of our own.

'Henry, I tell you that, for the first time in our married life, I saw that Gail was really *house-proud*! When she found out that she was pregnant she was overjoyed, and soon became so wrapped up in that happy fact that she no longer busied herself so much with the house. Not that Gail neglected any of the basic necessary housework – but our doctor – Ronnie Mead, you remember – pointed out that this being her first pregnancy, she should take things a bit easier.

'After all, Gail isn't all that young to be having her first baby – thirty-three this October – and though her pregnancy posed no serious problems, it called for a common-sense approach. So Gail eased up on the strictness of her routine and a local girl came in to help her out with the housework, three times a week.

'Of course, we've still not brought the whole of the house into use – and a number of upstairs rooms we keep locked and empty – but there is still enough space left for our needs to warrant quite hard work, just to keep it all clean, and all those good oak doors and that splendid panelling and joinery – well! As you know, Henry, this type of house was built when help was no problem to find – today you need every labour-saving device there is, just to keep things going.

'It was about then that I got the big Spencer project under way, and, naturally, I had to spend quite a lot of time at the final planning conferences, and then, of course, as soon as construction started, I was always dashing off to the site at Carmel. On previous trips into LA or up to San Francisco, I had been quite happy to leave Gail in the house alone – in fact she was so wrapped up in the place that she told me it didn't worry her a bit. Besides, the gardener didn't leave until dark and the daily help used to stay on until dinner. So really Gail was only alone in the house from about eight-thirty at night until eight in the morning, when the gardener arrived.

'Besides, Gail is a first-rate shot at "Skeet", and I've got a well-stocked gun cabinet, which she well knows how to use. Then there's the TV and hi-fi, the video-tape and all the other junk that we surround ourselves with, plus my library, which I've only just got straightened out – and, of course, those long heart-to-heart telephone calls that she makes to her sister in Santa Barbara – so there didn't seem to be much cause to worry, especially as Asgaard shuts up at night like a miniature fortress!

'I suppose I was much too busy and contented to realize what was happening, until one night I came home and found Gail in floods of tears. Naturally, being male, I put it down to the pregnancy, and I was completely taken by surprise when she suddenly blurted out: "John – would you be very angry – if we sold this house?"

'I couldn't believe my ears! It seemed so crazy. After all, it was her enthusiasm when we found the house that had made up my mind to buy it there and then. I really was flabbergasted when Gail told me she felt that there was something evil about the house – that she found the place oppressive – menacing – unbearable! It all came as a complete shock to me!

'The terrible thing was that Gail's obvious fear communicated itself to me, and I started to think about the previous owner – the old lady who was found dead by her cleaner – and I remembered the rumour going around at the time, that she had been trying to clean the chandelier in the hall, late at night, and had fallen from a ladder. It sounded such a crazy story that I had discounted it, but Gail's terrors brought it back to my mind and I found myself getting the jumps. More than that, I found myself looking at the house in a new and sinister light. Suddenly, I felt – and please don't say I'm mad! – I was *convinced* that the house resented me! Oh, Christ! What on earth has gone wrong, Henry?'

My poor friend's eyes peered anxiously at me from his white, drawn face, and my heart went out to him. I chose my words carefully as I answered: 'John, I want you to try and understand that the things I'm going to tell you may only have an indirect bearing on what has been happening – and that there are probably a whole host of reasons why you both feel this way about the house – all perfectly natural.

'When I dowsed for your well site, I picked up something that made me feel uneasy and, since then, I've learned one or two things about the builder of the house which may have a bearing on what you both seem to have picked up. None of it is horrific – you must trust me for that, because I am able to judge these matters – but the man who designed the house and supervised its construction was an eccentric, and there's so much of the aura of his personality still lingering about the house that you may somehow have clashed with that.

'What I'm trying to say is that I'm sure that it's all a question of your being over-worked and not realizing how tired you are. Frankly, John, you look exhausted. Also, being alone, and naturally being concerned about the coming baby, has preyed on Gail's nerves. Both of you are interacting with the other, and the house being fairly loaded with atmosphere has affected you as well. Thus the net result seems to be a vicious circle of loneliness – strain – worry – an isolated and unusual house – it has all added up to a slight paranoia – nothing serious – but worrying!

'Look, John, if it will help, I'll come up the day after tomorrow – I just can't before. I'll get my urgent business done during the next forty-eight hours, and stay over with you for a week or so, and together we'll get this nonsense ironed out. OK?'

My friend's pathetic gratitude went through me like a knife; and, in spite of my deliberately positive approach, I knew that I was in for a difficult time – in fact I felt badly about the whole thing. I wouldn't hear of him staying at the club that night, but insisted that he occupied my guest-room, and we both 'phoned Gail to tell her not to worry. John had got the woman who helped them – Mrs Delrey, a kind-hearted Mexican-Irish lady, who was as strong as an ox – to spend the night with Gail while he had come down to Los Angeles in a despairing attempt to find me.

Gail sounded tired, but happy to hear my voice, and obviously relieved that I was coming up to see them within a couple of days. John reassured her, and his own much more relaxed attitude must have cheered her up as well.

The next morning he drove back home, having taken a couple of days off from the Spencer project, and I set about clearing up things at my end.

Actually I had done most of my work that needed finishing in the first day, and that night I put a 'phone call through to England to someone who I knew could help me – and through me, God willing, the Bartletts.

Dom Robert Petitpierre was the exorcist of the Church of England – which, when you think about it, is a strange thing for a Benedictine monk to be. This remarkable, sensible and gentle scholar I had met some time before, at his headquarters at Nashdom Abbey, just outside London, and found him to be, in every way, a joy to know. With his wry sense of humour and extraordinary courage, he had often succeeded in ridding houses, and the people who lived in them, of the presence of negative forces – or, as he called them, the Powers of Evil. I knew that somehow I would get help from this quarter, and I wasn't wrong.

Dom Robert was away, but his associate told me that

there was a Benedictine living near Los Angeles who could help me, and, only an hour later, I was talking by 'phone to Dom Francis Morland. In view of the urgency of my call this good man agreed to meet me right away and the next morning he arrived, in the car that I had sent for him.

As soon as I shook his hand, I knew that I had been guided to the right person, and, as he sat opposite me, with his powerful black-robed figure leaning eagerly forward, and his dark eyes glowing with enthusiasm, I felt that like Dom Robert, here was a Warrior of Light.

'There have been many cases,' he said with a quiet authority, 'where the disturbances in a house or apartment have been traced to the lingering aura of a long-dead previous owner – some unfortunate entity that had extreme reluctance to leave the surroundings of its previous life. In other words, an earth-bound soul, locked into the material environment that we call the earth plane.

'Certain people, like Sir Wilfred Blunt, the English poet, author and explorer, had themselves buried in mausoleums near their homes, apparently to lock their psyches into the environment of their earthly homes – perhaps with the motive of serving those who inherited their goods after them. That's one positive aspect of this sort of thing, but, somehow, in the case of your friends' house, I don't feel that this is the situation.

'Then there was William Beckford, another English savant of an earlier period, who built Fonthill Abbey – a huge folly near Stonehenge – and another strange building near Bath. When he died he was embalmed and entombed on a small island in the middle of an ornamental lake in its garden.

'Both these men understood a great deal about dynastic succession and the influences that can be exerted on posterity *after death*, and, in Beckford's case, I cannot believe that it was for unselfish motives.

'In Lenin's case – one can so interpret the embalming of

the Father of the Revolution – there were the subsequent visitations by millions of people, who have made his tomb the object of pilgrimage and worship and I believe there is a very sinister aspect to the whole business.

'No matter how you look at the motives that possibly dictate these actions, I feel that for the dead to influence the course of the destinies of the living is neither right nor healthy. Thus I believe that your diagnosis is correct and that your friend – Mr Mellows, isn't it? – is right. His story of the subterranean mausoleum may well be the root of the matter. I'm certain that is what you dowsed.

'Now, as to how you can help your friends. I can't come up right away to perform a full exorcism – though that will only be a temporary measure. The real solution is to remove the embalmed body, with all due respect and dignity, and re-inter the corpse in some quiet and peaceful consecrated spot, and then clear out the grounds, in the spiritual sense, and fill in the mausoleum itself.

'In the meantime, go with my blessing and help your friends to remove themselves – temporarily – from the atmosphere of the place. You tell me that this will be no great hardship financially, and in their present nervous state, which is, of course, highly receptive to influences of evil, they would be well advised to leave, otherwise the unborn child may suffer.

'I'm sorry, but that is my considered advice. Since I am called out on these missions almost as often as the Fire Service, I will leave you this crucifix of wood from the Mount of Olives, and this small phial of Holy Water, which I have consecrated. I would give you a part of the Host – but I must get my Bishop's permission to part with that and, regretfully, he is away on a world-wide ecumenical mission. Strange, isn't it? A jet-set bishop!

'I shall, of course, as soon as I can, come and perform the full exorcism, but at least you won't be unprepared. And now, my son, let us pray.'

Then and there, in the drawing-room of my apartment in Los Angeles, this positive, kindly soul blessed me and my mission, and I left for Asgaard with a more resolute and humbly confident heart than I had had before he came to help me.

The drive up the Pacific Highway would, under normal circumstances, have taken me about two hours or so, but owing to a sudden heavy storm, the road had been narrowed to a single track, either way, by a serious landslide from the overhanging cliffs above.

It must have been around nine o'clock at night when I finally turned off the Highway and, in blinding rain, started along the tarmac part of the road leading up the winding valley to the Bartletts' house. For a time, when the rain became torrential, I actually had to stop the car altogether, and it was far later than I had reckoned, so that I was becoming deeply concerned about my friends, whom I could imagine were now wondering whether I was ever going to come.

To cap it all, the unmade part of their approach road was now a muddy torrent of water, draining down the narrow canyon, and my car was not designed for this type of work. Slithering along the quagmire of the track, it slipped uncontrollably into the ditch and stopped altogether. I'd been expecting it, so there was no real damage done, but it meant either my sitting unprofitably in the warmth and shelter of the car, or making a sodden dash for it along the three hundred or so yards remaining to the gates of Asgaard. Metaphorically girding my loins, I took advantage of a short lull in the downpour, and staggered groggily up the slushy mess of a road until I arrived, in a filthy temper and soaking wet with a renewed cloud-burst, to find the imposing gates wide open. Once over the gravelled threshold I quickly made a crunching beeline for the Ionic portico and yanked hard on the iron bell-pull.

The storm had built itself up again into a reasonable

facsimile of a Hollywood 'B' movie and, as I waited impatiently at the door, I almost expected Bela Lugosi to answer my summons. When the bolts eased back and the door at last swung open, I was as shocked at the sight of John's face as if I had been confronted by Boris Karloff himself. My friend looked ghastly, and, as I stumbled inside, he shut the door with a resounding bang and shot home the bolts as if he were under some terrible siege.

'Thank God,' he said simply, 'thank God you've come!'

He helped me off with my coat and, wordlessly, apart from that fervent greeting, led me by torchlight into the drawing-room, which was lit by copious candlelight and the orange flames of a log fire. Obviously the storm had cut off the house's electricity supply. But in spite of the warmth and the comforting dance of the flames, an ominous chill seemed to permeate the beautifully-proportioned room; and the sight of poor Gail, weeping softly and shivering as she huddled in front of the fire, was stark evidence of the presence of fear. I could almost taste the cloying mustiness of its aura as it hung there, filling the room with the smell of death.

I comforted Gail, who seemed on the verge of a complete breakdown, while John poured me brandy to warm my shivering body – and, believe me, that cold wasn't all caused by the raging storm outside and the failed electrical supply within. Unless you have been subjected to that type of paralysing fear, nothing will ever convey to you what it is like. You'll just have to take my word for it – I was absolutely terrified.

Until I started praying! I'm not a religious man – that is to say, I'm not a conventional churchgoer. Funerals I avoid like the plague, and weddings and christenings I attend more out of respectful affection for the participants than for the religious significance of the occasion. However, I do believe implicitly in the power of prayer, just as I

believe, equally firmly, in the power of evil. I happen to be
convinced that good will always conquer evil, in the way
that constructive and creative thoughts will always banish
destructive thoughts – so long as you make the effort to
bring this about.

For a minute or two the destructive powers loose that
night had me on the run, then, all of a sudden, I got good
and mad at the forces of darkness. I found myself praying
for help and, immediately, the conviction grew in me that
whatever happened we would, all three, come out of this
alive and well. I also had a growing feeling that I was an
instrument – a channel – that night for the light and, with
that becoming a certainty, I stood up and spoke out in a
clear voice.

I don't remember what I said – something about the
three of us being together and that there was nothing to
fear. But the effect on Gail and John was extraordinary.
They stopped shivering and clung together, so that the
three of us made a strange little group, in a way symbolic
of a father protecting and comforting two children in the
face of some nameless terror.

The response of the storm seemed more furious than
ever. The wind had risen to a peak, savagely battering the
house and rattling the leaded lights of the upstairs windows,
and driving the rain before it in torrential sheets. Yet,
suddenly, we seemed to have come out of the awful helpless
feeling of despair that had paralysed us, and my thoughts
were now positive and full of Dom Francis's warm presence,
and some of his infinite faith.

'Don't worry,' I said. 'This bloody jinx is going to be
beaten – we're going to win hands down – let's just get
things in perspective. So, there's a filthy storm outside!
Big deal! The electricity's failed – big excitement!

'Come on, Gail! There's that beautiful baby to think of –
nothing is going to touch *that*! I flatly refuse to accept what's
apparently going on here tonight. I don't give a damn for

any influence that is trying to hurt us. We're too strong for
it and we've got the light on our side.

'You are my dearest friends! We really love each other –
and there's nothing negative which can beat that! So come
on, Gail! John! Corny as it may sound, the family that
prays together, stays together: "Our Father, who art in
Heaven –" '

Stumbling at first, and then with growing vigour till we
were almost defiantly shouting the words, we said The
Lord's Prayer. A prayer which is far older than Christianity,
and which has its origins in the great religions of light that
preceded the Christian era – and its effect that night was as
magical as ever. The house seemed to shake in fury, but we
were strong and unafraid. I held the crucifix high over our
heads, and the small phial of consecrated water in the other
hand.

I knew we had to get out, right away, because the fabric
of the house couldn't take much more of that extraordinary
storm. All my instincts as a builder told me that the whole
place was becoming unsafe. The very foundations seemed
to be moving, as though a landslide was starting, or an
earth tremor was building up in the rocks below the house.

'The Fall of the House of Usher' – that phrase beat in my
brain, not as some spectral warning, conjured up by the
parallel situations of the storm-wracked Bartlett house and
that monstrous creation of the fevered brain of Edgar
Allan Poe, but as an urgent indication that now was the
time to get out.

At that moment the house began to move – John and I
could hear the groaning of the roof timbers and the ceiling
beams – while, beneath us, a hollow boom told of the start
of the collapse of the cellars, perhaps even the breakdown
of the octagonal mausoleum, if indeed one existed below
the house. There was a wild, distant clattering of tiles
wrenched loose and slithering down the steeply-pitched
roofs, and then, over our heads, the great crystal chandelier

started to swing – at first with a gentle tinkling sound and
an almost imperceptible sway, and then faster and faster,
till the frenzied clashing of the cut glass made a crazy
accompaniment to its wild pendulum swings.

Gail shrieked as a great gust of wind rushed down the
chimney and out of the fireplace, jetting a dense, swirling
mass of soot that plunged the room into darkness.

Choking and spluttering, and holding Gail firmly between us, John and I made for the door. As we reached it,
the whole building seemed to rear up in the air, and a
rumbling roar shook the heavily timbered oak floor of the
hall.

'Get out!' I shrieked. 'We must get out of here! The
whole damned place is coming down!'

We had reached the front door, which had burst open
and was banging crazily against the wall, when the staircase
began to break up, the heavy oak bannisters exploding out-
wards and the long, dark, polished wooden balustrade
plunging down on to the tiled floor below.

Gail fainted, and John bundled her over his shoulder as
we struggled out through the portals into the rain-lashed
night. For a moment I looked back, to catch a glimpse of
the panelling tearing away from the walls of the entrance
hall, and the huge gyrating crystal chandelier crunching
loose from its massive ceiling fixtures and crashing down to
explode into flying glass shards on the tiles below. Then I
concentrated on fighting our way down the gravel drive,
under the wildly swaying yew trees. Twice during our
stumbling headlong flight, tall trees splintered and fell in a
tangle of twisted branches right across our path. All but
blinded by the whiplash of the rain and buffeted by the
screeching wind, we somehow reached the gates, one of
which lay wrenched clean off its hinges. Out on to the
quagmire of muddy sludge that was once the hard-packed
dirt road, we splashed and lurched, too breathless for
speech, our hearts nearly bursting in our heaving chests.

At last I saw the car outlined in the glare of a lightning flash. Throwing ourselves forward, we wrenched open the doors and carefully lowered the unconscious Gail on to the back seat. While John wrapped her freezing body in a thick car rug, I got the engine going, and though I couldn't get the wheels to grip in the thick slime of the ditch, we at least had power, light and warmth.

Beyond the lashing tops of the distant yew trees, I saw a red glow, and realized that the house must have burst into flames, probably from the blazing logs of the drawing-room fire and the explosive clouds of soot which had billowed out into the room. Helpless to do anything about it, and with a strange feeling of relief, we watched the flames rise high into the storm, followed by great boiling clouds of black oily smoke which swirled upwards to meet with the low, racing storm clouds.

Dawn found us asleep in the depths of exhaustion, and, as we woke to the mildest of clear winter mornings, we all three found ourselves praying in gratitude for our safe deliverance. It was the fire that brought help to us, in the form of the Highway Patrol helicopter, which had been making a survey of the storm damage.

Gail was lifted off to the warmth and care of the nearest hospital, while John and I got the car out of the ditch with the aid of a police car, summoned by the crew of the 'chopper'.

Well, there you have it! A strange story, by any standards!

Gail and John had their baby – a beautiful little girl – and I am the proud godfather. The insurance paid up in full, and John and I designed and built a worthy successor to the destroyed Asgaard, but this time it was sited just outside Carmel.

The insurance assessor put the total destruction down to a combination of the freak storm and a quite severe seismic disturbance in the area, with the collapse of an underground cavern beneath the house as the primary cause of its ruin. Dom Francis and I have our own theory as to the cause of that disastrous night's work – but then, surely, everyone is entitled to his own beliefs.

I am of the opinion that Paul Harrington impressed his powerful and jealous love of order on to the house, as he built, furnished and cherished it. People who came into possession of Asgaard, as long as they also cherished and fanatically preserved the ordered beauty and proportion of it all, were completely in tune with the spirit of Harrington, locked beneath them in the octagonal mausoleum, of whose existence I am now convinced. The forthcoming baby – a rival cherished love – was the catalyst that let loose all the dark forces of a jealous hate, and the natural elements did the dreadful rest.

When the mausoleum collapsed in that final earth tremor, Harrington's presence ceased to hold Asgaard in its inflexible grip, and the building was destroyed in the final catharsis.

On the other hand, the insurance assessor put forward a perfectly logical explanation. As they say: 'You pays yer money and you takes yer choice.'

Especially if you are *house-proud*.

Sanctuary

THE HIGH-KEENING WIND scudded across the jagged, wolf-grey plateau, shrieking its fury like a flock of demented gulls.

The man, muffled obscurely in his ice-rimmed quilted parka, leaned heavily on a long yellow stave, his frosted gloves clutching the shepherd's crook handle in desperate exhaustion. Wearily, for the hundredth time since he had emerged from the ragged tree line two hundred feet below, the wind-whipped figure raised his snow goggles and scanned the massive bulk of the snow-shrouded mountain peak before him. This colossal stone bastion thrust itself out of the tumbled surface of the high plateau like a gigantic foam-flecked whale bursting forth from a frozen sea.

The man's narrowed eyes, smarting with the intense cold, burned in his gaunt, ashen face as they took in the mad tumble of rocks at the foot of the huge peak. Slowly, with methodical thoroughness, they surveyed the savage desolation, until at last they focused on a series of huge rocks, with an obviously man-made complex of tall granite towers set above them, flush with the base of the mountain's peak.

The man grunted his exhausted satisfaction and, shrugging his bulging pack higher on to his broad shoulders, he stumbled forwards through the thin mountain air towards the distant buildings.

From a small window, set high up on the wall of the mountain fortress, a pair of equally interested eyes was following the approaching figure every determined step of the way. The powerful pair of modern binoculars contrasted strangely with the timeless cowled robes of the watching monk.

With a final gasping effort the traveller threw himself against the tall black wooden doors which broached the great wall of the keep, and felt them judder, echoingly, against his weight as he banged the crook of his stave on the weather-pitted surface of the great portals. The knocks died away in the hollow silence of the hidden courtyard beyond, and the traveller sensed rather than heard a shuffling movement towards the doors, as in a broken shout, he croaked out a single word:

'Sanctuary!'

The age-old cry for succour faded quickly away on the gusting wind, while the sound of a rasping bolt being withdrawn from a reluctant socket indicated the promptness of the reply.

With a grunt of relief, the frost-rimed traveller thrust himself through the slowly opening gates and, as they slammed shut behind him, leaned back against them with his arms flung wide as though he were crucified, until with an infinitely weary sigh, he slid down in an unconscious heap on to the smooth, worn flagstones of the inner courtyard.

At a signal from the monk who had opened the doors, two other robed and cowled figures approached the slumped figure, effortlessly picked him up and carried him through a low archway set into one of the great grey granite towers that made up the massive complex of the fortress-monastery.

The doorkeeper followed them inside and motioned silently towards a door leading off to the side of a long dark corridor. The two burdened monks passed through the portal and gently laid the traveller down on a starkly simple wooden bed, which stood against one wall of a monkish cell.

This small, narrow room was lit by an arched leaded window, high up on the outer wall, its only furnishings, beside the bed, were a wash basin in a wooden stand and a prie-dieu, which did secondary service as a low chair.

Signalling the monks to leave, the doorkeeper quietly shut the cell door after them and busied himself administering to the crumpled form of his unconscious guest. He gently stripped off the heavy, soaking-wet parka and the thick, oiled-wool sweater underneath, then he removed the padded outer snow boots and the lighter deerskin ones inside, which, with heavy sea boot stockings, had saved their wearer from frostbite. Lastly he pulled off the down-filled over-trousers and removed a final sweaty one-piece suit of thermolactyl underwear, without which the semi-frozen traveller would have slipped into the white snow-sleep of death.

While the monk washed and cared for his exhausted body, the traveller stirred in the depths of his sleep as a host of images crossed the inner screen of his mind – images that would have contrasted strangely with the stark simplicity of his present surroundings, had he been aware of them.

It was as though he were viewing a constantly changing film, edited without continuity or sense of reason, yet somehow connected in a crazy patchwork pattern, and lit with a brightness and clarity that almost hurt his inner eye. Utterly helpless to shut off the seemingly endless kaleidoscope of visions, the traveller watched and slept.

Scenes of childhood and past youth interchanged with
momentary glimpses of anguished adulthood; shrieks of
childish laughter became the high pitched screams of
tortured pain; the laughing mouth of a girl became fixed
into the rictus of death; and the twirling limbs of a ballet
dancer suddenly twitched limply, the dancer's body now
dancing at the end of a hangman's rope. A flower opened,
in slow motion, and turned into the flame-riven rose of an
exploding grenade, while endless columns of marching
jack-booted men moved like robots before a leader seen
only in silhouette. Faster and faster the grim montage of
images flickered and dissolved, till they whirled down together into a bottomless black pit of unconsciousness.

Even on that profound plane of forgetfulness, the conscious mind of the sleeping traveller gave a loud moaning
gasp, and the doorkeeper's gentle hand stroked the sweating
head with a calming touch until the strained, haggard face
of the sanctuary-seeker lost its harsh lines and relaxed into
a calm serenity.

So these unlikely companions passed the long night
together – one deeply sleeping, the other watching and
soothing.

The savage dawn of the high plateau bathed the battle-
mented walls of the ancient monastery with a yellowish-
grey light that picked out the eroded crenellations with
pin-sharp shadows. The sheer might of this colossal
fortress proclaimed its origin and the majesty of its Templar
Knight builders to the unheeding, rock-strewn wilderness
before it. Raised, stone on massive stone, by the pride and
arrogance of the Templars, this long-forgotten and un-
chronicled monument to their knowledge had successfully
withstood the raging high-altitude tempests for five
hundred years.

The misty dawn light soon found the small, arched
window of the cell and, with growing intensity, outlined
the sleeper, so that he stirred restlessly on the plain wooden

pallet bed, while his watcher dozed fitfully, slumped on the prie-dieu chair beside him.

A gentle knocking at the cell door summoned the monk to wakefulness. He stretched and moved almost silently to the door. It opened with the faintest of metallic sighs from the ancient iron hinges.

In silence the newcomer, a tall monk with the cowl of his robe over his shaven head, handed the doorkeeper a wooden tray containing food and drink, and then, after the other had placed it on the prie-dieu, exchanged some complex signs with him.

The doorkeeper nodded and, as a bell sounded, both monks paused and then dropped to their knees as though struck down by some invisible hand. From their lips came a low murmuring as their hands gently rattled worn wooden rosaries over their fingers.

The bell sounded again – a high echoing note that gave no indication of how far off the belfry was situated, but seemed to issue from some part of the monastery a long way above them. As the sound died away on the rising wind outside, the monks rose from their orisons and silently parted company.

The doorkeeper resumed his vigil beside the traveller's bed just as the man woke, his eyes taking a brief moment to become accustomed to the brightening dawn light which was now filling the cell. His voice, rusty with sleep, again spoke only one word, but this time it was formed as a question:

'Sanctuary?'

The doorkeeper nodded and, with a craggy hand, pushed back the cowl which he had placed over his head for the prayers. His countenance, until now hidden in the darkness of the cell or concealed below the cowl, glowed softly in the golden light of the morning sun, revealed in all its strength.

The face of the traveller, which on waking had resumed

its anxious, drawn expression, gave a clear indication of
how vitally important his question was. As he read the
answer in the worldly-wise grey eyes of the doorkeeper,
his taut mouth relaxed into a dry-lipped smile, and he lay
back against the pillows, breathing evenly with deep lung-
filling movements of his powerful chest.

The monk indicated the tray of food and drink on the
prie-dieu and conveyed, by signs, that the traveller should
refresh himself. The naked man sat up in bed and the doorkeeper picked up and rested the laden tray on the bed, then
smiled and silently left the cell, closing the door after him.

While the traveller slowly and, with a discipline distilled
from long practice, determinedly ate a meal of thick broth
and scone bread and sipped the clear mountain spring
water, his mind was going over the details of what he must
soon say, to persuade whoever was in charge of this remote
monastery to allow him to remain there.

He had scarcely finished his meal when the monk returned, carrying a robe and a warm woollen undershirt
over one arm, while he held a pair of strong leather sandals
in his other hand. The doorkeeper indicated that he should
now dress himself and then follow him. The traveller complied with his silent instructions as deliberately as he had
eaten the much-needed meal, and finally nodded that he was
ready. Without further delay they left the cell and padded
down the long dark corridor towards a tall heavy door at
the end.

As they approached the archway that framed the door
the dark oaken panel swung silently open, as though of its
own accord, but actually at the touch of another monk
beyond the door, who had observed their arrival through a
small barred Judas-hole.

The doorkeeper was used to the golden blaze of light
that suddenly filled the stone corridor, and had automatically
cowled his eyes against it, but it took the traveller completely by surprise, temporarily blinding him to the details

of the great, sun-filled space beyond. He felt the door-keeper's arm firmly grasp his shoulder and guide him into a high vaulted hall, like that of some great manor house, blazingly lit by the morning sun streaming through a long low arched window, which opened out on to a stone balcony perched at a giddy height on the precipitously sheer face of the outer wall of the monastery.

As his eyes became accustomed to the glare, the traveller barely glanced at the magnificently frescoed walls of the great room. Though he noted the richly carved refectory table and the beautifully crafted benches and chairs which surrounded it, his gaze was irresistibly drawn towards the figure silhouetted starkly against the burnished golden light which flooded in.

The long, cowled abbot's robes emphasized the unusual height and broad, powerful shoulders of the man who turned to face him, signing to the doorkeeper to leave them as he did so. As the door of the great room closed behind the monk, the abbot spoke.

'Welcome,' he said in a deep, penetrating voice. 'You are refreshed.' This came as a statement rather than a question.

The traveller hesitated before replying, taken aback for a moment by the abbot's accentless mastery of his native language. How could the abbot possibly know his real nationality?

'My deep gratitude for all your help,' he finally answered.

'You have come a long way,' continued the abbot, again as a statement of fact.

'From the other end of the world. It has been difficult.' The traveller paused. 'But to gain sanctuary with you here makes any effort worthwhile.'

'We will only grant you temporary sanctuary –' The abbot deliberately lingered on the last two words, '– until we hear your full story. Only then can we finally decide whether you are to be granted indefinite sanctuary.'

'I understand,' the traveller nodded vigorously.

'Then please begin.' The abbot gestured with his large, powerful right hand, indicating that the traveller should seat himself in a heavy, carved chair in front of him, while he settled himself back into the depths of a massive wooden canopied throne, of ancient craftsmanship. With his face already cowled and now deep in the shadows of the great throne, the abbot made an ominous figure, as of one sitting in judgment.

'Everything will depend on your absolute truthfulness. Hide nothing from us! Your secrets will be quite safe here – one way or the other.'

The traveller hesitated as he considered the abbot's last words. Were they a veiled threat? Then he spoke:

'My name is of no consequence, or I have many. For this reason I am known as "Legion". My background is also of no import since by my language you know my country of origin. I swear to you that I am speaking my birth tongue – though there are others which, like yourself, I have totally mastered. That gives you the clue to my profession.

'When I was still at school I showed these aptitudes – among others, for I was also a strong athlete; and my ambitions, even then, must have been obvious. It was there that I was contacted, interviewed, considered and finally chosen for training in my country's Intelligence Service.

'My preliminary training was rigorous and, as I had been orphaned early in my life and had no other family commitments or contacts, I was soon placed in a highly specialized conditioning environment, far away from my previous home. Here my training became even more demanding as my instructors' confidence in my potential increased, and as the scope of the accomplishments that they conditioned into me expanded more and more.

'After three years of intensive work I became highly proficient in a number of languages, adroit in the use of complex intelligence techniques and a master of memory recall in technical subjects. Another two years brought me further skills in the use of explosives and sabotage techniques, and well practised skill with a number of firearms and other weapons. In that time I also perfected my languages and was thoroughly instructed in codes and cyphers, radio and other means of communication. By the age of twenty I had successfully assassinated my first target and, three months later I sabotaged a large power plant in a distant country – an ally of our enemy.

'The next ten years gave me an almost unique experience of every facet of cold war techniques, and during that time I became one of my country's three top intelligence operatives. Shortly afterwards, the other two met with fatal accidents, which left the field clear for me as top operative in our service.

'It was then that, by order of our Chief of Intelligence, I was retired from active service. I was considered to be too valuable to risk losing – and I was appointed Head of Training (Tactics).

'Over the next three years I developed new and more advanced techniques, which I had been perfecting for some time, and, at the end of that period, I was promoted from Tactical Training to become Second-in-Command of Overall Strategic Intelligence Planning. It was at this point, when everything seemed set for my next move to the summit of my career, that I made the first mistake of my life.'

The traveller paused and the abbot waited in silence for him to continue.

'I learned a great secret – or rather the final secret – the one piece of knowledge that, as Supreme Head of the Service, I could safely have possessed but which, as Second-in-Command, I could never be allowed to know and still be permitted to live. I had stumbled on the secret which only the top Intelligence Chiefs, throughout the world's most powerful nations could safely keep – for their own mutual protection.'

The abbot nodded, slowly, deep within the shadows of
the canopied throne.

'I had found out that all Intelligence organizations are
totally unnecessary. With modern satellite and overfly
infra-red techniques, the position of every ship, submarine,
tank, rocket, gun and even each individually armed soldier
is known, pinpointed, computerized and plotted automatically! Therefore, while there is a need for top electronic
engineers to operate and maintain such sophisticated fully-
automatic self-computerized equipment, there is no real
need for espionage agencies as such, or for the highly-
trained agents themselves. The new computers in service
have made them all – even the chiefs – totally redundant.

'Such knowledge in the hands of a chief executive-in-
command of a country's Intelligence service is safe enough
– even his opponents, who also possess such knowledge,
would never allow it to be released, as they would automatically destroy themselves. Redundant operatives with
highly specialized knowledge are immediately eliminated.

'The position is virtually a stalemate – political and actual
suicide for all, if such a secret ever leaked out! No careers!
No pensions! And above all – no power! So the ultimate
secret was safe in a chief's hands – for every Head of Intelligence has a hot line to all his counterparts throughout
the world, and they already knew that only by their mutual
silence could they guarantee their mutual survival!

'But –' Here the traveller paused again, '– for a Second-
in-Command to possess such knowledge, was the most
effective means of signing his own immediate death warrant,
should he be found out and it was inevitable that this would
be the case. Only the Chief of Intelligence is not regularly
interrogated with sophisticated and totally effective lie-
detectors. As Second-in-Command, I would have failed my
next routine interrogation. I had to move quickly and,
somehow, hide myself – not only from my own Chief but

also from the Chiefs of every other top Intelligence Service on the earth.

'I had already considered the possibility of killing my own Chief, but the chance of doing so successfully and not being caught were minimal in the short time before the next vital routine interrogation.

'I had already heard of the existence of your monastery and knew that it was safe – being unknown, except to the one man who had failed to gain sanctuary with you, and whom I had been pursuing for some time as a renegade operative. Before he died he told me about you. For that matter, he told me everything he knew, for that was part of my briefing and my skill at ultimate interrogation did the rest. Then he died – quickly!

'When I returned, I reported everything to my Chief except the fact of your existence – for, by exercising complete control during mental interrogation I have found that one can hold back knowledge from the interrogator – if he does not already share that knowledge!

'This, then, was the reason why I could safely face interrogation by my Chief on this subject, but not on the subject of the ultimate secret – which, naturally, he already knew. So I was able to retain this vital bit of information – of the existence of an ultimate place of sanctury and it was this knowledge that governed my plan to escape.

'I started by arranging a fake fatal accident, substituting a double, whom I had carefully selected for the purpose; and by this ruse, I was able to delay the subsequent search until the forensic evidence revealed the truth. I covered my tracks with every skill that I had acquired, making my way by car, small boat, private plane – with yet another arranged accident, involving two charred bodies, which made identification that much harder and gained me more time.

'I lay low for a short while and then, when the opportunity arose, took another sea trip in a small chartered fishing boat, which I later sank, paddling ashore in an inflatable dinghy.

'After further changes of route – some back-tracking – and the use of other techniques such as plastic surgery to my face and fingerprints – which, of course, necessitated the subsequent elimination of the surgeon in question – at last I had placed sufficient time and distance between myself and my international pursuers, who by this time had of course been alerted as part of the mutual-protection plan. I had become the top target for a number of seek-and-destroy missions, undertaken by the specialist operatives of each of the powers involved.

'It is only here, the whereabouts of which I am convinced is wholly unknown, that I am safe.

'The strain of this totally unexpected turn of events has given me an absolutely different viewpoint of life, and its ultimate purpose, and I am willing, and indeed eager, to accept your way of life and to be guided to whatever goal you may require me to seek. My skills are considerable and I am completely in your hands and at your service. I believe such service – total servitude – to be the object of your order, and that is what I am now willing to accept, as the form of my future life.'

After the traveller had finished, the abbot sat silently in the concealing shadows of the great throne. At last he spoke, slowly and with a careful choice of words:

'Your story has the absolute ring of truth – like an unflawed bell. I will consider your request for indefinite sanctuary, and your declaration of willingness to accept complete servitude.

'You will now return to your cell and await the outcome of our deliberations. The vows of our order include, among others, that of silence so from now on, you will communicate with the other brethren by signs alone! That is all! Go in peace!'

The traveller bowed and walked resignedly to the door, only his unshaven head proclaiming him to be in any way different from the doorkeeper, who had now reappeared, summoned by a bell, and was holding the door open for him to pass through.

The monk closed the door behind the traveller, shutting the golden light off from the dark corridor beyond, and waited for further instructions from the abbot, who had risen from the shadows of the canopied throne and walked quietly over to the long window, where he stood looking out over the balcony at the desolate vastness of the great plateau below. For a long while he remained in silent contemplation, his huge figure once more silhouetted against the golden morning light. At last he broke the silence. 'Give him sanctuary! Indefinitely!'

The doorkeeper inclined his head and turned to go, but hesitated as the abbot continued, half musing to himself and half addressing the monk!

'Strange how, eventually, they all come here! And each of them has much the same story to tell. The arrogant rise to power and then comes the first mistake, and the resultant fall into terror and pursuit.

'How much they fear their organizations! How terrified they are by them, whether they be C.I.A., K.G.B., Bundesnachreitdienst, S.I.S., Triad or Mafia or even some giant monolithic business corporation! How they fear them! And how stupid that fear is, when the only *real* thing to fear on this earth is our brotherhood and – above all – me!'

The deep, sonorous voice stopped – and then broke into a low, infinitely menacing laugh, which grew in power, echoing through the vaulted hall and spilling out over the massive battlements, until it was lost in the keening whine of the wild winds that endlessly buffeted the secret fortress, that unknown place which commanded the high plateau and from its obscurity, the wide world below.

The Beautiful People

IN CERTAIN BEAUTIFUL PARTS of the world live the beautiful people.

They live out their beautiful lives in beautiful homes, wearing beautiful clothes while they eat beautiful food and drink beautiful drinks.

There is, of course, nothing new in being beautiful people. Ever since civilization became based on sound monetary economic systems, groups of beautiful people have gathered together in beautiful places to enjoy each others' beautiful conversation and to make love to each others' beautiful partners. The Persians, the Egyptians, the Chinese, the Greeks, the Indians, the Romans and, latterly, the Twentieth Century Global Jet-set have, each in turn, congregated – one could almost say, huddled together – to enjoy their beautiful existence.

I have lived for a short time among some of these beautiful people. I say 'among' rather than 'with' because I am not a beautiful person; but I amuse these beautiful people and they even tell me that, had I been gifted with their brand of talented success – that is to say, monetary success – I might just have qualified for inclusion in their beautiful set. That is, of course, if my success had made me as rich as they are – in other words, if I were beautifully wealthy.

From time to time these beautiful people suffer a tragic set-back in their beautiful lives, such as when the servants walk out, or the caviar goes bad in the deep freeze, or they break the last bottle of a favourite brand of champagne. But they usually manage to survive these catastrophes and to come up smiling – beautifully, of course.

As a matter of fact, the beautiful people are very adaptable and can adjust themselves to meet tragedy head-on, and to weather sadness and personal loss, with amazing resilience – provided that the unfortunate circumstances happen to people other than themselves.

One incident that sticks out in my mind among the fleeting memories I have of this beautiful life, concerns four of these beautiful people.

They were marriage partners and skilled in all aspects of their beautiful lives. Occasionally they would make beautiful extra-marital love to each other – sometimes even together, in a beautiful foursome. Four beautiful people movingly woven into a beautiful pattern.

One night these two beautiful couples climbed into a beautiful car and went for a drive along a beautiful road, to a beautiful little town with a beautiful view. There, in a beautiful restaurant, they ate a beautiful meal and drank lots of beautiful wines.

On the way home, along the beautiful road, the beautiful couples changed partners and made beautiful love to each other as they went along. Then, at a particularly beautiful part of the beautiful road, they ran head-on into an ugly truck, driven by an ugly man, and broke their beautiful necks.

Now, although there was a perfectly good undertaker in the beautiful town around which the beautiful people lived, a specialist embalmer of great skill was specially flown out at enormous expense to do justice to their broken corpses.

This he did, carefully embalming and recreating each beautiful body so that each of the beautiful faces once again bore beautiful smiles.

When he had finished, this most expensive of all undertakers smiled a smile of complete satisfaction.

'Beautiful job!' he said. 'Mind you, it was easy! After all, there wasn't anything in them!'